LABRADOR ON THE LAWN

'Over there,' Mandy said, standing on tiptoe and pointing over the flowerbed.

James shaded his eyes with one hand. Only the glossy black tip of Blackie's tail could be seen, waving like a banner as it disappeared round the side of the cottage.

'Honestly!' said James, exasperated. 'Will that dog *ever* learn to do as he's told?'

They pushed their way out of the overgrown part of the garden and ran down the stone path that led along the side of the cottage. But Mandy stopped dead when she got to the corner.

There were *two* dogs on the lawn! Standing nose-to-nose with Blackie was a sleek, golden-haired Labrador.

Animal Ark series

Holiday Specials

Plus

LUCY DANIELS

Labrador
— on the —
Lawn

Illustrations by Ann Baum

*Hodder
Children's
Books*

a division of Hodder Headline Limited

Special thanks to Ingrid Maitland

Animal Ark is a trademark of Working Partners Limited
Text copyright © 2003 Working Partners Limited
Created by Working Partners Limited, London W6 0QT
Illustrations copyright © 2003 Ann Baum

First published in Great Britain in 2003
by Hodder Children's Books

For more information about Animal Ark,
please contact www.animalark.co.uk

10 9 8 7 6 5 4 3 2

A Catalogue record for this book is available from
the British Library

ISBN 0 340 87388 4

Typeset in Baskerville by Avon DataSet Ltd,
Bidford-on-Avon, Warwickshire

Printed and bound in Great Britain by
Clays Ltd, St Ives plc

The paper and board used in this paperback by Hodder Children's
Books are natural recyclable products made from wood grown in
sustainable forests. The manufacturing processes conform to the
environmental regulations of the country of origin.

Hodder Children's Books
a division of Hodder Headline Limited
338 Euston Road
London NW1 3BH

One

'There it is!' Mandy Hope gasped as the car rounded a bend in the road. 'The lake! Look, James!'

'Where?' asked James, leaning forward and fumbling with his glasses. His dog, Blackie, sat between James and Mandy on the back seat. The Labrador's broad, whiskery muzzle lifted to the breeze as Mandy opened the window.

'Budge over,' James instructed his dog, who obligingly swapped places. He peered excitedly out of the window on Mandy's side. A vast stretch of slate-grey water stretched for as far as they could see along a wide, tree-lined valley.

'Wow,' said James. 'It's huge!'

Mandy's dad pulled the Land-rover to the side of the road and switched off the engine.

'Oh, it's gorgeous,' sighed Emily Hope, winding down the passenger window and taking a deep breath of cool air. 'Look, Adam,' she added, as her husband got out of the car, 'you can see the Langdales from here.' She pointed to a ridge of dramatic grey crags at the northern tip of the lake.

'And a yacht or two!' Adam Hope said longingly, gazing at the white sails that dotted the lake and giving the impressive mountains only a quick glance.

Mandy and James scrambled out of the car. Blackie bounded after them and James just managed to grab his collar before he took off down the steep bank.

'Poor Blackie!' Mandy smiled, smoothing the dog's sleek black head. 'We know you've been dying to get out and explore for an hour.'

'And so have you two!' laughed Mr Hope, adding, 'There's not much further to go now.'

They stood in silence for a moment, drinking in the scene. Beams of sunlight bounced off the silvery surface of Windermere. Mandy knew that the lake, at ten-and-a-half miles long, was the longest in England, but she hadn't been able to imagine its beauty. She thought it seemed peaceful and dramatic at the same time. She turned to her father, her eyes shining. 'I can't wait to get there.'

'Well, we'd better get on, then,' said Mr Hope, turning back purposefully towards the Land-rover. 'We're only a few miles from our cottage, according to the map.'

Mandy settled back into the hot car, feeling excitement fizz inside her. Their journey had begun that morning in their home village of Welford in Yorkshire. The Hopes had rented a cottage in the tiny village of Graythwaite, about three miles west of Windermere. James had been invited to come along to share the week's holiday, with Blackie as well, of course.

The visit to Cumbria had been Mandy's mum's idea. She and Mandy's father were vets who ran their own surgery, called Animal Ark. They'd had a very busy first half of the year.

'We need to get away,' Mrs Hope had suggested one Sunday morning, after a particularly challenging session trying to remove a hook and fishing line from the throat of an angry badger.

'Not anywhere far or exotic . . . just a nice, peaceful break.'

This was Mandy's first visit to the Lake District, so she and James had looked it up on the Internet. With the mountains, forests and waterfalls, it looked the perfect place for rambling with a good friend and his adventurous and lovable dog. Mandy slipped an arm round Blackie's shoulders and gave him a hug. His tongue lolled, making him look as though he was smiling. The tip of his tail twitched happily, because there wasn't room on the back seat to stand up and wag it properly.

Blackie's ears shot up as the road they were on led them into the deep shade of Grizedale Forest, as if he was listening to something. Mandy began to wonder if there were any animals peering back at them.

'Is the forest home to any particular animals, Mr Hope?' James raised his voice to be heard above the noise of the engine.

'Quite a few mammals, James,' replied Mandy's dad. 'I expect we'll be lucky enough to see roe deer, red squirrels, maybe a badger . . . and rabbits, of course.'

'Wonderful birds, too,' added Mrs Hope.

'Woodpeckers and jays, nuthatches and goldcrests and warblers.'

'And sheep,' said Adam Hope. 'Lots and lots of sheep. This is sheep farming country.'

James looked across Mandy and raised his eyebrows. They were both mad about animals.

'This is going to be fun,' Mandy smiled.

'You bet,' James responded. Blackie licked James's cheek and he wiped his face with the back of his hand. 'Get off, Blackie!' he protested. The dog sighed and tried to lie down but there wasn't room. As he shuffled around, he trod heavily on Mandy's hand.

'Ouch,' she said. 'Mum, I think Blackie needs to get out.'

'I'm sure you're right,' said Mrs Hope, turning to look at the panting Labrador.

Adam Hope nodded. 'Yes,' he said. 'But we can't let him loose just here. This is a fairly busy road. Let's go on for a bit and see if we can find a safe place for him to stretch his legs.'

Blackie was in luck. Just a mile further on, the trees ended, and Mr Hope was able to turn on to a narrow dirt road leading between some fields. He followed the twin tracks to a thicket of tall pines. Blackie began to whimper with delight.

'All right, all right,' said James, as Blackie began to scratch at the door. 'Can I let him out, Mr Hope?'

'It should be OK,' said Mandy's dad.

'It looks like pasture,' Emily Hope remarked, looking round, 'but I can't see a single sheep. That's good.'

'Let him go, James!' Mandy pleaded. Blackie's black nose twitched at the enticing smells coming from the lush grass around the car. He had managed to stand up on the seat, and was wagging his tail so hard it swiped at Mandy's face. James flung open the door and, with one bound, Blackie was out and following his eager nose into the undergrowth.

Emily Hope got out and stretched, while, from the back of the car, Mr Hope found the remains of the picnic lunch they'd had earlier. 'A chocolate biscuit, rather melted,' he announced, 'and two cans of drink. Anyone?'

'No thanks, Dad,' Mandy grinned, watching Blackie rolling happily in the dry grass.

'Keep an eye on him, won't you, James?' Mrs Hope warned, looking at Blackie. 'Farmers round here are bound to be very protective of their flocks. Dogs that worry sheep can be shot.'

'Yikes,' said James, pushing his glasses higher up on his nose. 'What a horrible thought.' He called to his dog, a look of concern on his face.

But Blackie wasn't listening. He was standing stock still, his ears pricked and one paw raised. His nose was raised to the breeze.

'Blackie!' said James, more sternly. 'Come here.'

Mr Hope put up a hand to shade his eyes from the sun. 'He's spotted something,' he said.

'Look, James!' cried Mandy, climbing on to the bumper of the car to get a better view. 'Rabbits!'

And with that, Blackie was off, streaking away over the crest of the hill, barking joyfully.

James groaned and set off in pursuit. 'I'll get him back,' he called as he broke into a trot. Mandy ran with him. She had no fear for the rabbits. She was certain that Blackie would be too slow to catch them. The big softie only wanted to play. James picked up speed and she raced beside him, yelling the dog's name.

In the pasture that stretched away on the other side of the hill, Mandy saw the rabbits scatter. One by one, they hopped neatly into nearby burrows in the ground and disappeared. Blackie pounced on a burrow, his tail wagging. He barked loudly and pushed his nose into the hole.

'Blackie!' puffed James, one hand pressed to his side as he gasped for breath.

And then Mandy's heart skipped a beat. Just beyond the burrow was a flock of sheep. She caught hold of James's sleeve to alert him. 'Hang on,' she said. 'Don't yell at him any more.'

James turned to her and frowned. 'Why not?' he panted.

Mandy pointed. The sheep had raised their heads and were staring balefully at the big dog. They began to bleat and fuss, shifting warily and turning in confused circles. The panic spread through the flock like wildfire, and a few began to run.

Blackie backed out of the rabbit hole and looked at the sheep. He appeared to be sizing them up, and Mandy's heart began to thump harder.

'James . . . he wouldn't . . . would he?' she gasped.

James groaned again. 'I hope not,' he said. But he sounded worried. Then he groaned even louder. 'Oh no, now we're in trouble – look!'

As the flock began to scatter, James had seen a man crouching. He had been attending to a sheep, which lay on its side at his feet. He let the animal go and it went lumbering off. Then he stood up and looked about him.

James and Mandy froze. 'Has he got a gun?' James whispered.

'I don't know,' Mandy whispered back. She looked back up the hill for her parents, but she couldn't see the tree or the Land-rover from where she was.

Blackie's attention switched from the sheep to the stranger who had popped up among them. He wagged his tail in greeting and trotted towards the man to say hello.

Mandy tried waving at the farmer, a smile on her face.

'Clear off!' he shouted. 'I don't want that dog frightening my flock. Call him back, will you?'

'I'm very sorry,' Mandy shouted back. 'He wouldn't do any harm, honestly.'

'Can't take that chance, I'm afraid.' The farmer waved his arms at Blackie, who stopped. He seemed puzzled by the firm tone of the man's voice. His tail drooped and his ears went down.

'Blackie!' James used his sternest voice. 'Here – now!'

The Labrador turned and walked back to James.

He looked rather sorry for himself, and Mandy's heart melted.

'Don't scold him, James,' she said. 'Let's just go, as quickly as we can.'

'You were lucky this time,' remarked Adam Hope, as they rejoined the main road. 'We must make absolutely sure Blackie doesn't go wandering off again.'

James was flushed pink from his dash over the hill. He was still cross with Blackie, who had relaxed on the back seat, looking out of the window as though he hadn't a care in the world.

'I hope the cottage garden is fenced,' said Emily Hope. 'I didn't think to ask when I booked it through the agency.'

'Who owns the cottage?' Mandy asked.

'I've no idea,' replied her mother. 'The woman at the agency didn't say. I think the owners are just letting it out for the summer.'

'This is the road,' said Mr Hope, spotting a signpost. 'Sunny Brow Lane.'

Mrs Hope looked at the map. 'We want number four,' she reminded him.

Mandy sat up straight. She couldn't wait to see

the cottage. It had such a lovely name – Laurel Cottage. She hoped it would be really old, filled with interesting nooks and crannies.

She wasn't going to be disappointed, she realised, as her dad pulled up outside a tiny whitewashed cottage that stood on its own in a rambling, flower-filled garden. Grizedale Forest stretched out on all sides, with a silver glimmer just through the trees below showing where the lake was.

Ivy covered the walls of the cottage, reaching almost to the chimney. The split front door, painted butter yellow, and tiny, wooden-framed windows gave it the appearance of a doll's house.

'Oh!' Mandy gasped. 'It's lovely!'

'Will we all fit in it, do you think?' James frowned. 'It looks rather small.'

'It has three bedrooms,' said Adam Hope, looking doubtful.

'We'll be fine,' Mrs Hope told them. 'Come on, let's unpack and put the kettle on.'

Mandy jumped out and ran up to the front door. It had a rusted old brass knocker shaped like a lion's claw. James let it fall with a resounding thud.

'I've got the key,' Mrs Hope said. 'And it really will be a squash if there's anyone else staying here!

Let's leave Blackie in the car for a bit, just until we investigate the garden.'

James nodded. 'Good idea.' From the back seat of the Land-rover, Blackie howled his disapproval at being left behind.

Mandy unlocked the front door and went in. She found herself in a little hall, leading to a living room, with a flagstone floor and shaggy rugs, a big friendly-looking fireplace and a mantelpiece piled with interesting ornaments. A framed painting of an otter hung over the fireplace. Mandy went closer to admire it. The animal was poised on a rock in a river, looking intently into its depths. Mandy smiled. She loved otters. But there was more to see in the cottage, and she raced after James, up a steep wooden staircase to the bedrooms above.

'One,' Mandy counted, pushing open a wooden door. 'This has got a double bed so it can be mum and dad's room. Two, small but nice . . . and right opposite, bedroom number three! Which one would you like, James?'

'This one, please,' said James, admiring a small painting of a fleet of yachts on the wall above the bed.

'Good,' said Mandy happily, 'because I like the one overlooking the front garden.'

'That's settled then,' James said. 'I'd better go and see if it's OK to let Blackie out. He'll be hot in the car.'

'I'll come with you,' Mandy offered.

Mrs Hope was in the kitchen, filling the kettle, and Mandy's dad was just coming through the front door with some of the luggage from the boot of the car.

'I'll help in a minute, Mr Hope,' James said cheerfully. 'I'll just see that it's safe to let Blackie out.'

'Fine, James,' Mr Hope grinned. 'Great little place, isn't it?'

'It's brilliant,' Mandy smiled. 'It's a storybook cottage.'

'Are you coming, Mandy?' called James.

'Yes!' said Mandy, squeezing past her father and out of the door.

James had begun to pick his way between two overgrown flowerbeds. He and Mandy walked slowly round the edge of the garden, checking there was enough of a fence to stop Blackie leaping off into the meadow.

'There's a jungle of thorny bushes here,' Mandy said. 'I don't think Blackie would try to get through this!'

'I don't know,' James frowned. 'He's bright enough to work out how to escape if he wants to.'

'And bright enough to have squeezed out of a car window!' said Mandy, laughing.

'What!' said James. 'Where is he?'

'Over there,' Mandy said, standing on tiptoe and pointing over the flowerbed.

James shaded his eyes with one hand. Only the glossy black tip of Blackie's tail could be seen, waving like a banner as it disappeared round the side of the cottage.

'Honestly!' said James, exasperated. 'Will that dog *ever* learn to do as he's told?' They pushed their way out of the overgrown part of the garden and ran down the stone path that led along the side of the cottage. But Mandy stopped dead when she got to the corner.

There were *two* dogs on the lawn! Standing nose-to-nose with Blackie was a sleek, golden-haired Labrador.

Two

'Now where did *you* come from?' Mandy whispered.

'It's another Labrador!' exclaimed James.

'I can see that! Isn't she beautiful?' Mandy declared.

'Not as nice as Blackie,' James responded loyally. 'But she's pretty, I'll give you that.'

The dog was slightly smaller than Blackie, with a narrow tapering face the colour of butter. She had darker markings around her caramel-coloured eyes, and her ears were pale gold.

Blackie stood stock still for a moment, staring at the strange dog. Then he wagged his tail hesitantly.

The golden Labrador lay down submissively. Blackie seemed a bit puzzled at first, but, as Mandy and James watched, the bigger dog's playful nature got the better of him. His whole body began to sway with the force of his wagging tail. He gave a little prance, then stretched down to sniff the dog's face.

'Uh-oh,' James said quietly. 'Do you suppose she'll mind Blackie being a pest? I mean, do you think they'll fight?'

'Fight!' Mandy echoed. 'That's not likely. Labradors are the best-natured dogs in the world, for a start, and secondly . . . it's a girl!' Mandy glanced at James and grinned.

The mystery dog was still lying on the lawn, her pale gold tail wagging gently. She waited patiently while Blackie circled her, sniffing at her coat. His inspection complete, Blackie seemed completely overcome with joy at finding a new friend. He rolled over on to his side, paddling all four paws at her like a puppy.

'You silly dog,' muttered James.

'They like each other!' Mandy declared happily. 'Come on, James. Let's go and say hello.'

The Labrador looked up as Mandy and James

approached. She cocked her head and her tail stopped wagging.

'Hang on, Mandy,' said James. 'She seems a bit wary. Shouldn't we wait till her owner turns up?'

'What if she doesn't have an owner?' Mandy pointed out. 'After all, there aren't any neighbours round here, and there were no cars parked in the lane. She might be lost.'

When they were just a couple of metres away, the Labrador stood up. She looked directly at Mandy, her brown eyes soft. She limped a single step, then stopped and raised one front paw.

'James! She's injured,' Mandy cried. She crouched on to her haunches, making herself small and unthreatening, the way her parents had taught her, and gently stretched out one hand. 'Hello, you lovely girl,' she said.

James was distracted by Blackie, who had bounded over to him and was standing on his back legs trying to lick James's face.

'Down!' James commanded, smoothing Blackie's head. He looked over to see how Mandy was getting on. Mandy was stroking the dog's head, still talking softly.

'You've hurt yourself,' she told her. 'You need help

with that paw, and you've come to the right place.'

'Do you think that she'll follow us into the cottage?' asked James.

'I'm not sure,' Mandy replied. 'She seems friendly enough but she's also a bit nervous.'

'We don't want her to run off,' mused James, who walked across the grass and knelt down beside Mandy to get a better look. The Labrador was in good condition, her coat sleek and shiny and her ribs well covered. 'She's not been going hungry,' he observed, pointing to her plump pink tummy.

'I don't know where she could suddenly have appeared from.' Mandy felt puzzled. She tried taking a closer look at the paw the dog was holding up, but the Labrador pulled away at once and warned Mandy off with a soft growl.

'She's really in pain!' Mandy exclaimed. 'James, will you go and fetch Mum or Dad? I'll stay here with her.'

'Right.' James sounded very purposeful. He backed away slowly so as not to startle the dog, then, when he was well clear, he sprinted for the back door to the cottage. Blackie stayed with Mandy and his new friend.

The yellow Labrador gazed after James as he disappeared indoors. Mandy tried to look at the underside of her paw, without going too close, but she couldn't see anything. She held the wriggling Blackie at arm's length, and was relieved when her father came striding out of the cottage, James hurrying behind him.

'What have we got here? I can't believe you've managed to find another animal in need of help just minutes after our arrival!'

Mandy nodded as her dad approached, walking

slowly so as not to alarm the dog. 'No collar,' he remarked, setting down his veterinary bag on the grass. He held out a gentle hand and the yellow Labrador looked up sorrowfully as Mr Hope bent over her.

'Poor girl,' he said soothingly. 'Will you let me see that paw?'

'I tried to have a look,' Mandy told her dad. 'But she wouldn't let me touch it.'

Adam Hope reached gently for the dog's foot. The Labrador snatched it away, but not before he'd seen enough to know what was needed. 'Wow, that's quite a cut she's got there. It must be very uncomfortable for her.'

'What are you going to do, Mr Hope?' James was standing a little way off, hanging on to Blackie.

'I'll have to give her a sedative, I think, to calm her. Then she'll let us bring her inside and treat her wound,' he said.

While Mr Hope prepared an injection, Mandy's mum arrived with a handful of Blackie's treats. 'What a gorgeous dog!' she exclaimed. 'I wonder where she came from?'

Blackie jumped out of James's grip and pushed his eager nose into Mrs Hope's palm. 'No, Blackie,' she laughed. 'These aren't for you.' James ran up and grabbed Blackie's collar again. The dog seemed determined to get as close to their visitor as he could!

Emily Hope gave the biscuits to Mandy, who offered one to the yellow Labrador. She stretched her neck out and accepted it gratefully. Her nose worked as she lay on the grass, looking for more.

'Oh, Mum, she's hungry, poor girl,' Mandy said.

'I expect she's been wandering around for a while,' said Mrs Hope. 'That doesn't look like a fresh wound. But her coat is in good condition so I shouldn't think she's a long-term stray.'

The Labrador was still busy sniffing for more biscuits, when Adam Hope gently slid his needle into the muscle at the back of her neck. As the syringe released the sedative drug, she looked round, surprised, then shook her head vigorously.

'Good,' said Mr Hope, straightening up. 'It won't be long before she's dozy enough to bring indoors. Then we'll see what we can do with that paw.'

It took just a few minutes before the golden Labrador began to get sleepy. Mandy stroked the top of her head. She could see the confusion in the dog's brown eyes and felt a pang of sympathy. She hoped the dog knew they only wanted to help.

'She's going all wobbly,' James whispered, as the Labrador struggled to stand up and took a faltering step. She flopped down on her side and stretched out with a long, contented sigh.

'Now,' said Emily Hope. 'Let's take her inside.'

Mr Hope bent down and scooped the Labrador into his arms. He held her round her chest and tail, and her chin rested on his arm.

Emily Hope had gone into the cottage ahead of them and spread several sheets of newspaper on the big wooden table in the kitchen. Mandy opened the kitchen door wide enough for Mr Hope to squeeze through with the dog lying in his arms. He laid her gently on the tabletop. In a moment, Blackie had his front paws on the table, craning his neck to sniff at her.

'I think we'd best keep Blackie out of the way, James – just for now,' said Emily Hope.

'Right,' said James, looping his fingers through Blackie's collar. 'I'll put him back in the car, shall I?'

Adam Hope nodded as he scrubbed his hands under a running tap at the kitchen sink.

'And make sure he can't get out of a window!' Mandy added with a smile, before turning her full attention to the Labrador on the table. Using a pair of small sterile scissors, Mrs Hope had started clipping the fur from between the pads on the dog's front paw. Tufts of soft yellow hair fell on to the newspaper, exposing a deep cut on the tender place just above the pad.

'That looks sore,' remarked Adam Hope. 'My guess is that she's made the cut worse by walking around on it. It'll need stitching.'

James slipped back into the kitchen. He stood beside Mandy and stroked the dog's head. She was awake, and blinked up at them, but she didn't seem to mind about the strangers attending to her paw.

'Sweet girl,' Mandy murmured, feeling how velvety her ears were. She helped her mother by taking the scissors from her when the fur had been clipped away, and watched as the cut was thoroughly cleaned with sterile liquid on gauze. Then Adam Hope stepped up with his needle threaded, ready to stitch the wound. First, Mandy knew, the dog would be given a shot of local anaesthetic, so she wouldn't feel any pain.

When Mandy's mum slipped a fine needle into

the paw, the Labrador appeared not to notice, but lay still, looking quite comfortable. Mandy kept a gentle hand on her head. She watched the strange loops of the needle and passed her father the scissors as each stitch was neatly finished and cut.

'There,' he said, when the last one was complete. 'A few antibiotics to make sure you don't have any infection, young lady, and you'll be as right as rain.'

Mr Hope heaved the Labrador into his arms again, and Mandy led the way into the sitting room to find a comfortable place where the dog could lie. 'Why don't we put her here?' she suggested, patting the rug that lay in front of the hearth.

The dog's head lolled as Mr Hope carefully laid her down and she sighed again, closing her eyes.

'I expect she'll want to sleep for a while, Mandy,' Mrs Hope called. She had rolled up the newspaper and was spraying disinfectant on to the kitchen table.

'OK,' Mandy replied. 'I'll just keep an eye on her, though.'

James sat on the floor beside Mandy. 'Where do you think she's come from?' he asked. 'And what are we going to do with her?'

'I can't think,' said Mandy. 'She's a beautiful dog. She must be somebody's pet. I'm sure someone out there is searching for her even now.'

'We should give her a name, just for the time she's here with us,' James suggested.

'Yes,' Mandy smiled. 'She's too lovely not to have a name. What do you think it should be?'

'How about Serena?' said James.

Mandy wrinkled her nose. 'Sounds like a name for a princess,' she teased. 'What about Goldie? She has such a wonderful golden coat, after all.'

'Goldie!' James said approvingly. 'Yes, that's it. Goldie.' He tried the name again. It seemed to suit the sleeping Labrador perfectly.

Adam Hope came in and lowered himself into an easy chair. He looked down at his patient. 'She couldn't be in better hands, that's for sure.' He smiled at Mandy and James. 'But what are we going to do with her now?'

'I think she's lost,' Mandy said.

'But what if she's been abandoned?' James looked worried. 'You know, dumped by someone who doesn't want her any more?'

'Well, whatever happened to her, she hasn't been alone for very long,' Mr Hope reassured him. 'She's in good condition, and that suggests to me that she's wandered away from her owners rather than been dumped.'

'We've decided to call her Goldie,' Mandy told him.

'Some of the locals might know of her,' suggested Emily Hope, coming in from the kitchen with two cups of tea. 'Why don't you and James walk into the village and ask around?'

'That's a great idea, Mum!' Mandy agreed. 'Is it OK if we go now?'

'I should think so. It's not very far,' Mr Hope said, looking at his watch. 'You could try asking at the post office first.'

'Yes!' James jumped up and Goldie's eyes flickered sleepily. Just then, a volley of shrill barking could be heard from the direction of the car.

'Oops, that's Blackie,' said James. 'He'd like a walk. Shall we take him along?'

Mrs Hope picked up Blackie's lead from a side table. 'You'd better take this,' she grinned. 'And don't let him off for a minute!'

James chuckled while Mandy tied the laces on her trainers. 'Which way is it?' she asked.

'You can't go wrong.' Emily Hope was looking at the map they had used to find the cottage. 'The village is back the way we came, right along this road, then left at the telephone box.'

'I know where you mean,' Mandy nodded.

Mr Hope handed Mandy some money. 'Will you buy a loaf of bread, love?' he asked. 'I'm sure the post office will have a village shop as well, like the one in Welford does.'

'Sure,' said Mandy. 'We'll do our best to find out something about Goldie as well and be back before it gets dark.'

James was already at the door. 'Come on, Mandy,' he called.

Mandy could tell he was as eager as she was to solve the mystery of Goldie's appearance on their lawn. She snatched up her jumper from the back of the chair. 'Right,' she said. 'Let's go.'

Three

Blackie was so pleased to be let out of the car that he jumped up with his paws on James's chest and tried to lick his nose. Then, as though he suddenly remembered the pretty golden Labrador he had met in the garden, he turned and raced back towards the cottage. Mandy and James chased after him.

'Hey! Come back here!' James shouted.

Blackie had come to a stop by the closed front door. He stood and looked up at James, his tail wagging hard. 'Blackie,' Mandy explained patiently, 'you're coming with us for a walk. You can't go in there. She's not very well.' She clipped the lead on to the dog's collar and handed it to James. Blackie followed at his heels.

It was a warm afternoon and the sky above was a clear blue. Mandy and James went out of the gate to the cottage and turned left down the narrow tarred road towards the village. Mandy hadn't realised how high up they were, but now she could see the towering peaks her mum had spoken of, and a ring of gentle green hills that spread magically all around them.

'There's the lake!' said James, stopping abruptly to point and making Blackie cough as the lead jerked tight.

'This is a great place,' Mandy said happily. Then, more seriously, she added, 'I just hope we can find Goldie's owner before too long.'

'We will,' James said with determination. 'She's such a beautiful dog. I'm sure somebody in Graythwaite will know her.'

After ten minutes, with James having to stop frequently while Blackie dragged him off to investigate a special scent along the side of the road, they rounded a corner to see the village before them. A pretty church stood at the far end of a long, narrow street. There were houses along either side of the road, and from where they were standing, Mandy could see two shops with big front windows that curved into the street.

'We'll make a start there,' said Mandy, heading for the familiar red sign that announced a post office.

The door was locked. A sign in the window read: 'Closed. Opening hours: 9am–1pm.'

'It's closed,' said James, disappointed. He rattled the door.

'Don't,' Mandy warned. 'We might set off an alarm or something.' She cupped her hands round her face to block out the glare from the sun and looked in. There wasn't anybody about. 'That's a shame,' she said.

She stepped back and noticed a photograph of an otter on a poster taped inside the window. She was immediately drawn to the small fuzzy head and beady bright eyes. The little animal lay on its back in water, its front paws touching over its chest. 'Another otter!' she said.

'Where?' James sounded surprised, and looked up and down the street.

'Not there, silly!' Mandy laughed. 'In there – on the poster.' She tapped lightly on the glass.

'Oh!' James looked in. 'It's a pup,' he said, grinning. 'I love otters.'

'So do I. They're *so* sweet,' Mandy smiled. 'Lakeside Otter Sanctuary,' she read aloud from the poster. 'A special environment set up for the rehabilitation of rescued otters.'

'Newly opened in Lakeside,' James read on. 'I wonder where that is?'

Mandy turned to him, her eyes wide with excitement. 'James!' she exclaimed. 'Lakeside's not far from here. I remember driving through it on the way to Windermere. We could ask Mum and Dad to take us there!'

'That would be great,' James agreed. Together they gazed at the poster, trying to make out the small writing along the bottom of the paper.

'Excuse me?'

Mandy jumped. A woman had quietly come up behind them. She wore a wide-brimmed straw hat and in her hand she held several postcards.

'Hello,' Mandy said brightly.

'Is it open?' the woman asked. 'The post office, I mean.'

'No,' James chipped in. 'We missed it. It shut at one o'clock.'

'Oh, dear, I did want to get these off today,' the woman said. 'I'll be back in Buckinghamshire before they reach my brother at this rate.'

'You're a visitor to the Lake District?' Mandy asked, hoping the woman wouldn't think her rude for prying. She hurried on with her question. 'You see, my friend and I have found a dog . . .'

'It's a Labrador,' James put in. 'A yellow Labrador.'

'And we don't know where it came from,' Mandy continued. 'We were hoping someone in the post office might be able to help us.'

The woman adjusted her hat and looked down at Blackie. 'Yellow?' she echoed, sounding puzzled.

Mandy grinned. 'Oh no, not *this* dog. This is Blackie. He belongs to my friend James.'

Blackie had found a small piece of waxy paper and was lying with it between his front paws, ripping it to shreds with his teeth. When he heard his name he sprang up. His tail began to thump happily and he strained on his leash to sniff the woman's hand. James tugged his dog back as she backed quickly away.

'I'm sorry,' she said. 'I'm not very good with dogs. I come out in a frightful rash from their fur, you see.'

'Oh dear,' said Mandy, quickly helping James to keep Blackie away. 'We'll let you go then.'

'I'm sorry I can't help,' the woman said, turning to leave. 'Perhaps you could try the bed and breakfast I'm staying in? Caleb's Cottage. It's just across the street.'

'Thanks,' Mandy smiled. At her feet, Blackie had snuffled up the last scrap of paper and was holding it in his mouth.

'Bye,' James called to the woman, while trying to pull the dirty wrapper out of Blackie's mouth. He straightened up, and frowned at his slimy fingers. 'Yuck,' he said, wiping his hand on his jeans.

'Let's try the bed and breakfast next,' Mandy said. 'I'll go in. You can wait here with Blackie, if you like?'

'Right,' James agreed.

Mandy crossed the road. There was very little traffic, even though it was the holiday season. She spotted a sign above an arched doorway reading, *Caleb's Cottage*. She pushed open the front door and found herself in a narrow hallway. There was a small white desk with a telephone on it but no one was about. Mandy wondered what to do. Should she call out?

'Can I help you?' said a voice.

Mandy jumped and turned. A young man wearing a green-and-white striped apron had appeared in a doorway. He dabbed his perspiring forehead with the sleeve of his shirt.

'I hope so,' Mandy began, feeling a little shy. 'I've come on holiday to Graythwaite with my parents.

We're staying for a week in Laurel Cottage and we've found a dog. It just appeared . . .'

'A dog?' he repeated, coming towards Mandy and looking interested. Her spirits rose.

'Yes, a yellow Labrador,' she confirmed. 'It's lost, we think . . .'

'I'd like to help,' he said kindly. 'I love dogs. I'm the new chef here. I'm from London and I haven't had a chance to meet any of the locals yet – or their dogs.'

'Oh,' Mandy said, her heart sinking.

'There's an RSPCA office here, I know that,' the young man went on helpfully. 'You could take the dog there. They'd put it in kennels for you, until they can find it a new home.'

'Thanks, but I think we'll go on trying to find her owner,' Mandy said.

'Well, good luck then.' The chef smiled at her. 'I'm sorry I couldn't help.'

'That's all right,' Mandy smiled back. 'Thanks, anyway.'

As she was waiting to cross the street to where James was waiting, she saw her friend wave to a boy pedalling away on a bicycle.

'Any luck?' James asked, as Mandy joined him.

Blackie wagged his tail and pushed a wet nose into the palm of her hand.

'No.' Mandy shook her head. 'I spoke to the chef but he's new here too.'

'I stopped a boy.' James pointed to the departing back of the cyclist as he sped off round the corner. 'He's camping with his family. He did say he'd seen a golden Labrador who belonged to one of the families on the site.'

'Hmm,' said Mandy. 'There's no telling if it might have been Goldie, though.'

'Hang on a minute. How about this for an idea?' James looked triumphant. 'Why don't we take a photograph of Goldie and pin copies all around the place?'

'That's a brilliant idea!' Mandy agreed. 'And we could make posters too! Come on, let's go back and do it right away.'

'Um, aren't we forgetting something?' James shook the loose change in his pocket.

Mandy looked blank, then suddenly remembered. 'The bread!'

Blackie seemed delighted to be on the move. He trotted ahead, pulling at his lead and looking round with great interest.

'Here's the shop. I'll go in,' James offered, handing Blackie's lead to Mandy. She gave him the money.

'Brown, please,' she told him.

'OK, and I might ask the person behind the counter if they know of Goldie, too.'

'Good thinking,' Mandy nodded her approval.

Blackie sat down again and sighed heavily. Mandy rumpled his ear. 'Not much of a walk for you, is it, boy?'

James was only a minute, and he came out of the shop shaking his head.

'What?' asked Mandy.

'I tried to ask, but the shop suddenly got very busy. I just didn't get a chance. There was a lot of pushing and shoving behind me.' He sounded frustrated.

Mandy smiled at him. 'Bad luck,' she said. 'Never mind. Let's go home and plan our poster campaign. I'm starving anyway. Aren't you?'

'Yes,' James agreed, taking Blackie's lead.

'And I'm dying to see how our lovely Goldie's getting on,' said Mandy.

*   *   *

As soon as James and Mandy arrived back at Laurel Cottage, Mrs Hope put her head round the door of the kitchen. 'Hi,' she said. 'Did anybody know anything about our mystery Labrador?'

'No.' Mandy handed her mum the bread, then kicked off her shoes.

'Nothing but tourists in the village,' added James, looking forlorn.

'Well, that's what we are, too,' Emily Hope smiled.

'How is she?' Mandy glanced at the hearthrug, but Goldie wasn't there. She looked back at her mother, puzzled.

'She's out in the garden with Dad,' said Mrs Hope. 'Go and say hello, if you like. Make sure Blackie doesn't knock her off her feet, James. She's not very steady yet.'

Mandy and James went out of the kitchen door. Blackie shook his head vigorously to make sure he was free of his lead, then scrambled after them.

Adam Hope was sitting on the lawn reading a book. From time to time, he looked up to watch the Labrador snuffling around him, limping heavily, with her injured paw held off the ground.

'Dad!' Mandy called. 'We're back.'

Mr Hope looked up and smiled. 'Did you find Goldie's owner?' he asked.

'No. We couldn't even find a person who *lives* here,' Mandy told him.

'That's the trouble,' said Mr Hope. 'At this time of year, locals are vastly outnumbered by tourists.'

'Uh-oh,' James said warningly. 'Look out . . .'

Blackie had spotted Goldie and was racing towards her. Then, just as Adam Hope got to his feet to try and prevent a collision, Blackie seemed to sense that pouncing on his friend wouldn't be a good idea. Instead, he lay down on his tummy and put his head on his paws, wagging his tail.

Goldie's ears pricked up. Hopping on her three good paws, she walked up to the black dog and stood over him. Blackie stood up to sniff at her chest, and turned in a circle, inviting her to join in a game.

'Hold your horses, young man.' Adam Hope stepped in and took hold of Blackie's collar. 'She's not well enough for a dance just yet.' James ran forward and hung on to his dog.

Mr Hope rummaged in the pocket of his shorts for a treat. 'It's best we go inside,' he said. 'She needs to rest that leg and I don't want her wandering off, either.'

Goldie limped after Adam Hope, her front paw held high. Blackie was happy to follow his new friend into the kitchen of the cottage. Mrs Hope had just put down a bowl of fresh water and both dogs lapped thirstily. When she was finished, Goldie went to the front door and wagged her tail expectantly, looking over her shoulder at them with pleading brown eyes.

'She wants to leave!' Mandy said sadly.

'Well, she can't,' Emily Hope shook her head firmly as she laid a steaming vegetable casserole on the kitchen table. 'She needs to rest, overnight at the very least. We'll make a plan in the morning. Come and have something to eat now.'

Mandy and James washed their hands and sat down at the table. Blackie had found his favourite toy, a rubber bone that had been well chewed. He padded over to the door and presented it to Goldie, sweetly laying it at her paws.

'Ah,' Mandy sighed. 'They're so lovely together.'

'Mandy and I have decided to make a poster that will help us find Goldie's owner,' announced James.

'That's a good idea,' said Emily Hope.

'We thought we might make a few of them,' Mandy added. 'We'll stick them up around the village.'

'We thought we could take a few photographs of her, too,' James said.

'Yes,' said Mandy. 'Somebody might recognise her.'

'Do you think that her owners are still around?' James asked. 'I mean, they could have been tourists too, and now they might have gone back to where they came from.'

'I can't believe that anyone would give up a dog like Goldie quite so easily,' said Mr Hope.

'She's a real mystery,' Mandy remarked.

'We'll find her owners,' said Emily Hope, spooning some casserole on to James's plate. 'I'm sure we will.'

Mandy turned to look at the two Labradors. Blackie was lying beside Goldie on the front doormat.

'I hope so,' she said. 'I *really* hope so.'

After supper, Mandy and James made a bed for Goldie in the kitchen. The Labrador seemed restless and unsure, and Blackie hovered over her, as though he was worried. Time and time again, Goldie hobbled to the front door, looking up expectantly at Mandy with big, sad eyes.

'No, girl,' Mandy said, smoothing her head. 'You must stay here, just until we can find out where you belong.'

Finally, with an air of defeat, Goldie settled down on the blanket Mandy had spread out. As Mandy sat with her, the dog's eyes started to close.

'Go to sleep,' Mandy whispered, letting her hand travel down the dog's silky coat, all the way to the base of her tail.

'Goodnight, Goldie.' James bent down to pat her. Blackie gave a final prance, still trying to coax his friend into a game of chase. But Goldie had fallen asleep, and James led him away.

Adam and Emily Hope were looking at guidebooks in the sitting room, making notes on a pad of paper.

'I'd like to set aside a day for a spot of sailing,' Mr Hope was saying when Mandy came in.

'Goldie's asleep,' she announced. 'James has taken Blackie upstairs to his room.'

'Good idea,' Mrs Hope smiled. 'We don't want any mad games in the night.'

Mandy yawned. 'Are there sheets for the beds, Mum?'

'It's all done, love,' her mother replied. 'Have a good night and I expect we'll all be up bright and early to see how Goldie is.'

Mandy nodded. 'She'll be fine,' she said. 'She's a good girl. But I really hope we find her owner soon. Somebody must be missing her badly!'

Four

Mandy woke to the sound of scratching. It took her several seconds to work out from which direction in the cottage the noise was coming, and what it could be.

And then she realised.

'Blackie!' she chuckled. She looked at her watch. It was six-thirty, early enough for her to do her best to try and keep him quiet, and allow her parents to sleep on. She slipped out of bed and across the hall to James's room. The wooden floorboards felt cold and slippery under her feet. Blackie stopped scratching as he sensed her approach and gave a particularly heart-rending whimper of frustration.

'James!' Mandy hissed, opening the door just a crack. Blackie's brown eyes looked up at her. James had closed the curtains across his window and the room was still quite dark. All Mandy could see was a tuft of brown hair sticking out from a tangle of sheets and blankets.

Blackie was thrilled to see her. Mandy put out her hands to him and he licked her fingers. 'Silly boy,' she said, tickling him under his chin. 'I'm sure you're longing to see Goldie, but you must be quiet! We'll let you out in a minute.' Mandy prodded a bump under the blanket. 'Wake up, James.'

The bump groaned. A hand appeared and groped on the bedside table for the pair of glasses. James put them on and sat up, blinking, looking around as if he couldn't remember where on earth he was.

'Blackie's going to wake the whole house,' Mandy told him, grinning. 'He wants to go downstairs and find Goldie.'

'What time is it?' James mumbled.

'Early – six-thirty,' said Mandy, pulling Blackie away from the door. He'd managed to leave a claw mark on the paintwork already. 'James, *do* something! Shall I let him out?'

'We'd better check on Goldie first,' James said sensibly. 'We don't want Blackie leaping on her and knocking her over if she's still feeling poorly.'

'No,' Mandy agreed. 'But if we leave him in here, he'll scratch the door to shreds.'

James got out of bed and reached for Blackie's lead. 'There,' he said, clipping it on to Blackie's collar. 'Come on, let's all go downstairs and see how the patient is.'

The staircase creaked loudly and Blackie coughed as he strained at the lead. Mandy was certain her mother and father would be wide awake by now, but it couldn't be helped. In the kitchen, Goldie was drinking from the water bowl. She was delicately poised on three legs, holding her front paw high off the floor. She jumped and staggered when James, Mandy and Blackie burst through the door.

Blackie was overjoyed to see the Labrador again, but James held him back on a short lead. 'Easy, boy,' he said, sympathetically.

'It's all right, Goldie,' Mandy crooned, stroking her. 'It's only us. How are you feeling?'

Goldie wagged her tail and lay down on her side. Mandy looked at her raised paw and gasped. 'James! She undid all of the stitches. Look!'

Goldie's cut had opened up again, and had started to bleed.

James knelt beside her, one arm outstretched to stop Blackie pouncing on her. 'Yikes,' he said.

'Will you call my dad?' asked Mandy. 'I'll stay with her.'

Without a word, James scrambled to his feet and pounded noisily up the stairs.

Mandy's head swivelled between Goldie and Blackie as she anxiously tried to keep an eye on both. Goldie had begun licking her injured paw and Blackie's brown eyes were fixed longingly on his new friend. *Why won't you come and play?* he seemed to be asking.

Adam Hope appeared in his dressing gown. 'So!' he said. 'You've managed to spoil my fine handiwork have you, young lady?'

Goldie's tail twitched in a hesitant greeting. She sat down and looked up at Mr Hope with a sheepish expression.

He bent over her and gently lifted her paw. 'Yep,'

he said cheerfully. 'You've made short work of that lot of stitches. What are we going to do with you?' Goldie thumped her tail on the floor.

Emily Hope came downstairs and had a look at Goldie's paw, too. Peering over her parents' shoulders, Mandy could see a little dried blood on the fur where the wound had been bleeding again.

'Can't we just bandage it up?' asked James.

Mrs Hope shook her head. 'The wound is gaping a bit, James. It'll need to be stitched again.'

'But she'll only rip them out!' Mandy said.

'You could be right about that.' Adam Hope shook his head. He soothed the Labrador with his hand. 'And we haven't got a cone with us . . .'

'What's a cone?' asked James, who had both arms round Blackie's chest as the black Labrador strained to get closer to Goldie.

'You know, James,' said Mandy. 'It looks like an upturned bucket. Dogs wear it like a collar so they can't lick the places they shouldn't.'

'Oh, yes,' James nodded. 'Did you say you *haven't* got one, Mr Hope?' He sounded doubtful. Mandy's dad always travelled with his vet's bag, which was stuffed with a never-ending supply of veterinary bits and pieces for any emergency.

'It's not the sort of thing I carry around with me, I'm afraid,' Mr Hope admitted, smiling.

'A lampshade!' Mandy said loudly, making Goldie lift her head and prick up her ears.

James stared at her. 'Yes?' he prompted.

'I spotted one on a shelf in the cupboard in my bedroom! We could use that, couldn't we?' Mandy was delighted with her suggestion.

'Well, at a push . . .' Emily Hope looked doubtful as she filled the kettle. 'We'll have to replace it, of course.'

'Oh, Mum, we will,' Mandy said earnestly. 'I'm sure the owners of the cottage wouldn't mind, not if they knew how important it is.'

'In your cupboard? I'll go and get it,' said James, getting up and pulling Blackie with him.

Goldie put her head down again and sighed. Her foot was clearly causing her some discomfort because she seemed reluctant to move about. Mandy stroked her until James reappeared, holding a battered-looking but sturdy cardboard lampshade. It was bright pink, with a loud floral pattern.

Adam Hope looked up. 'Hmm,' he said. 'You know, I think that in terms of size and fit, this will do the job perfectly! We'll have to cut it open, then fold it round her neck so that it fits snugly.'

'I'm so glad,' said Mandy. She took the shade from James. 'It doesn't weigh much, so it won't be too uncomfortable for her to wear. Dad, what can James and I do to help?'

'Well, you and mum and James can start by magically turning this lampshade into a cone to fit over Goldie's head. I'll sedate her and stitch her up all over again,' said Mr Hope. 'But first, I'll drink a drop of my tea.'

'I'll take Blackie out for a bit,' said James. 'Should I look in the garage for something to cut the lampshade open?'

'Thanks, James,' Mrs Hope smiled. 'That would be a great help. Strangely enough, I haven't brought any pruning shears with me!'

Mandy helped her father prepare the kitchen table for Goldie's second operation. She found a newspaper and spread it out, then set out a pile of sterile wipes and some cotton wool. Meanwhile Adam Hope went to fetch his toolbox from the car.

'You're a great assistant,' said Emily Hope, handing Mandy a mug of hot chocolate.

'Look what I found!' James shot through the kitchen door, tugged along by Blackie. 'It's a hacksaw. It was lying on a shelf in the garage.' James blew and dust flew off the small saw in all directions.

Mandy sneezed. 'Great!' she said. 'Let's cut up the lampshade.'

'I'll make the first hole, shall I?' suggested Mrs Hope, picking up a kitchen knife. She eased the sharp point of the knife through the cardboard. It gave easily, and she waggled the knife to widen the hole. When it was large enough, James took over with the hacksaw, pushing it back and forth to saw a clean line from top to bottom.

'Neat!' Mandy said approvingly. 'What's next?'

'This is my bit,' said Mr Hope, brandishing a screwdriver he'd retrieved from the toolbox. He turned on a ring of the gas cooker. James and Mandy watched with interest as he held the tip of the metal screwdriver in the flame, turning it until it was glowing white-hot. Even Blackie seemed interested, and stopped straining on his lead to reach Goldie.

Mandy held the lampshade at the wider end as her father instructed. He pressed the scalding screwdriver against the patterned cardboard. There was a sizzling sound and the sharp smell of burning. 'One small hole,' Adam Hope grinned. 'And now another . . .'

'But what're they for?' asked James.

'I'm going to thread some cloth bandage through each of the four holes and tie the lampshade to her collar,' he explained.

James looked puzzled. 'Goldie hasn't got a collar,' he pointed out.

'Not just now she hasn't,' Mr Hope smiled. 'Goldie will have to borrow Blackie's collar, if you don't mind, James?'

'Oh,' said James, adding, 'No, not at all.'

'We can buy Blackie another collar tomorrow morning,' Emily Hope told him. She and Mandy began to cut strips of bandage to thread into the holes round the edge of the lampshade.

'What a great cone,' Mandy declared, delighted with their team effort. At their feet, Goldie was steadily licking her wounded paw, reminding Mandy that the little Labrador still had another operation to face.

'Poor girl,' she said, bending down to stroke her. 'It'll soon be over.'

Emily Hope filled a syringe with sedative. As she approached, the dog flopped her head down with a big sigh, as though she knew exactly what to expect.

When it was all over, Goldie lay on the floor, sleeping off her sedative.

'Let's pop the lampshade on her now,' suggested Emily Hope. 'She's sleepy enough not to mind.'

Mandy went over to the dog and helped by holding the Labrador's head in both hands. It lolled in her palms and the weight of it surprised her. Goldie's eyelids drooped as Emily Hope folded the cardboard round Goldie's neck, closing it again into its original cone shape. Mr Hope threaded a strip of bandage through each of the holes and tied it firmly to Blackie's collar, which he had had to make smaller to fit Goldie's neck.

'There!' said Mandy's dad, stepping back to admire his handiwork.

'It looks a bit uncomfortable,' said James uncertainly. 'Not her paw. That lampshade thing, I mean.'

'It's called a cone,' Mandy reminded him. 'And I don't think Goldie will mind it too much. The flowers quite suit her!'

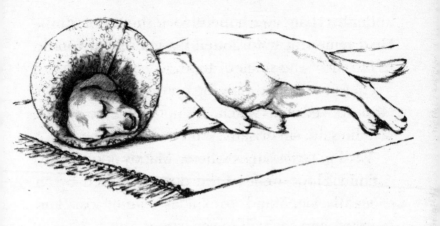

'Dogs get used to these sorts of things very quickly,' Adam Hope added.

Goldie's face was out of view, encased in the upturned lampshade. The weight of her head on the floor made the cone tilt and from within it came the sound of gentle snoring.

'I'd like to thank my team for their expert help with this morning's veterinary emergency,' announced Adam Hope, raising a glass of orange juice in a toast.

'A pleasure,' said James. He sat down at the kitchen table. 'I think we deserve a big breakfast after that!'

Mrs Hope, who was breaking eggs into a pan of sizzling butter, smiled at him. Blackie squeezed under his chair, ever hopeful for a shower of titbits. He'd temporarily forgotten his interest in Goldie in favour of the smell of food.

There was a loud rapping on the front door. Mr Hope looked at his watch. 'It's not even nine o'clock yet,' he said, surprised. 'Who could that be?'

'We don't *know* anyone here,' Mandy pointed out.

Emily Hope went to the door, followed by an eager Blackie. Mandy took a last bite of toast and scurried into the hall to see who it was.

'Hello?' Emily Hope said as she opened the door.

A young man stood on the doorstep. His hands were deep in the pockets of his jacket and he looked rather embarrassed. 'Good morning,' he said. 'I'm really sorry to disturb you so early on a Saturday morning. My name's Ben Sullivan.'

'Yes?' Mrs Hope sounded cautious. 'Can we help you?'

'My wife Sue and I used to live in this cottage,' he explained. 'We had a dog, and she's gone missing. I don't think for a moment she would be here but . . .'

Mandy's heart skipped a beat. *Goldie! Could this possibly be her owner?*

James appeared beside her. He tugged at her

sleeve. 'Hang on a minute. How do we know he's really Goldie's owner?' he whispered anxiously. 'I mean, he might be an imposter . . . a thief, or something.'

'Come in,' Emily Hope was saying. She stepped aside to let the visitor into the sitting room.

Mr Sullivan thanked her. 'Our dog's called Daisy,' he said. 'She's a golden—'

But before he could finish, there was a loud clattering and scrambling noise from the kitchen. The flowery lampshade came crashing through the door, cannoning off the door posts. Inside the cone, Goldie staggered against the wall.

'Daisy!' exclaimed Mr Sullivan. 'Where have you *been*? And what have you done to yourself?' He leaned down to welcome the dog with his arms wide open.

The Labrador tried to lick his face, but the cone made it impossible to reach. Ben Sullivan's fingers sank into Goldie's soft yellow fur as he stroked her, and Mandy's eyes filled with sudden, hot tears.

'She turned up on the lawn with a badly cut leg,' Emily Hope explained. 'My husband and I are both vets. We put a few stitches in her paw.'

'Thanks, that was really kind of you!' Mr Sullivan smiled broadly as he looked up at them.

Mandy glanced at James, a wave of relief washing over her. Goldie was really Daisy, and she had found her owner!

Mrs Hope led Ben Sullivan into the kitchen where Adam Hope was spreading marmalade on a slice of toast. He stood up and put out his hand. 'I can guess who you are,' he smiled, shaking Mr Sullivan's hand. 'Goldie took off out of the kitchen like a rocket when she heard your voice!'

'Daisy, Dad,' Mandy said softly. 'Her name is Daisy.'

Everyone warmly invited Mr Sullivan to stay to breakfast. Emily Hope brought a tray of tea into the sitting room, where Daisy lay with her cone resting on Ben's foot. Blackie had curled up as close to Daisy as he could get, as though sensing his friend would soon be gone.

'We called her Goldie,' Mandy told Ben, as she sat cross-legged on the floor with one hand on Daisy's flank. Ben Sullivan had really friendly eyes, she noticed, and a lot of curly brown hair.

'Sue and I got her when she was just eight weeks

old,' he said, smiling. 'She's so much a part of our family. We couldn't bear it when she disappeared.'

'What happened?' James prompted. 'How did she get out?'

'Our property is . . . rather big,' said Ben. 'It isn't exactly fenced. Daisy went off exploring soon after we moved away from here – she's rather independent and she's done it before. This time, she must have forgotten her way home, her *new* home, that is.'

'How long is it since she vanished?' asked Emily Hope.

'Two days.' Ben shook his head. 'We've been frantic. I wish I'd thought to come back to the cottage before now. It seemed like such a long way for Daisy to wander.'

'Where are you living now?' Mandy said. Then she drew in her breath so sharply that Blackie barked. Mr Sullivan had just taken off his light raincoat. On the T-shirt he wore underneath was a face that Mandy recognised instantly. It was the otter cub she'd seen on the poster in the post office window!

Ben looked at her in surprise. 'Our new house is about six miles away,' he said. 'In Lakeside.'

'I knew it!' Mandy leaped to her feet. 'We saw a poster with that otter on it in the post office window here.'

'Lakeside Otter Sanctuary? That's us,' Ben grinned. 'We've only been going a short while. It's been hard work, but very rewarding.'

'An otter sanctuary?' Mrs Hope opened her green eyes wide with interest.

'Yes,' Ben nodded, looking serious. 'It's been a dream of ours to manage a sanctuary for wildlife ever since we married. It seemed a dream that might just come true when my wife, Sue, inherited some money earlier this year.'

'That's wonderful,' Mandy breathed.

'So we decided to rent out this cottage and bought a piece of land we'd had our eye on for a long time,' Ben finished simply.

'In that case, you and you wife must be our temporary landlords?' said Mr Hope.

'I guess so!' Ben laughed, adding, 'And while I'm here, is everything up to scratch?'

'Great,' Adam Hope confirmed. 'Not that we've had a lot of time to inspect the place.' He pointed at Goldie, smiling. She was lying very quietly now, obviously delighted to be reunited with her owner.

'Is she going to be all right?' Ben asked.

'She's fine,' answered Mr Hope. 'She must have cut her foot on something sharp while she was exploring, that's all. I'll give you a few antibiotics to take with you, just in case she's picked up an infection.'

'You've been so good to her,' Mr Sullivan said, bending down to stroke his dog. 'And whose collar is this? It isn't Daisy's.'

'It's my dog, Blackie's,' James spoke up. 'We lent it to her so we could tie on that cone thing she's wearing,' he explained. 'Mr Hope stitched Daisy up, and she undid the stitches with her teeth. We used a lampshade we found upstairs, as it was an emergency.' He suddenly looked uncomfortable, and glanced at Mandy.

'How inventive!' Ben Sullivan laughed. 'I'll replace Blackie's collar for you. And don't worry about the lampshade. It's an ancient old thing, and I never liked it anyway!'

'Daisy was a great patient,' Mandy said.

'I can't thank you enough,' said Mr Sullivan, finishing his tea. 'I'd better get back to Sue and tell her the good news.' He stood up and pulled on his jacket.

'I'm very relieved you thought to come here,' said Emily Hope.

'So am I!' Ben replied, shaking Adam Hope's hand once again.

Mandy glanced at James. He raised his eyebrows at her and she guessed what he was thinking. Should they ask about the otters?

Before she could say anything, Ben spoke again. 'As a thank you for looking after Daisy, would you like to come out tomorrow and spend the day at the sanctuary with us?'

'Would we?' grinned James.

'We'd love it!' Mandy nodded.

Mr Sullivan delved in his coat pocket and produced a leaflet. 'This will tell you how to find us,' he said. 'We'd love to show you round.'

'That'll be great. Thanks,' said Adam Hope, taking the leaflet.

Mandy got down on her knees and looked into Daisy's eyes. The Labrador blinked sleepily back at her from inside her cone. 'It's time to go home, girl,' Mandy told her, rubbing under her chin. 'Your new home, that is. You don't live here any more, remember?' Daisy licked Mandy's hand.

'We'll miss you,' James said to the golden Labrador. 'Especially Blackie.'

'Bring Blackie tomorrow,' said Ben. 'I'm sure Daisy would love to see him.'

'Thanks.' Mandy gave Daisy one last pat as the dog got clumsily to her feet and tried to hurry to the front door ahead of Ben. It seemed she was determined not to be left behind. But she misjudged the width of the cone and collided with the door frame with a crash. Confused, she sat down and looked up at Ben for help.

'Oh, there'll be a few lessons to be learned with that thing on your head, Daisy,' said Ben.

Mandy soothed the dog and guided her through the door. 'Poor girl,' she murmured sympathetically. Daisy was a funny sight with the lampshade on her head, but Mandy tried to imagine how difficult it must be for her, not to be able to see exactly where she was going.

Outside, Daisy staggered about, getting in the way of Ben's legs. Whenever she wanted to look out sideways from the cone, she had to turn her whole body and if she wasn't bumping into things with the lampshade, she was treading on people's feet.

'She's not going to let you go without her, that's for sure,' smiled Emily Hope.

Ben Sullivan opened the car door and eased Daisy up on to the back seat. He waved. 'Thanks again,' he said.

Mandy waved back. 'See you tomorrow!' she called.

Five

It was hard not to keep looking at the big kitchen clock as Adam Hope made pancakes the next morning. Mandy had woken before the others and had sat at the window in her bedroom, looking out at the misty dawn and imagining the otter sanctuary. Time seemed to crawl by.

'Missed!' cried Mr Hope, scooping up a pancake from the floor before Blackie could get there. 'I'm not terribly good at this tossing business. Another one, Mandy?'

'I've had enough, Dad, thank you,' Mandy said.

'I'll have another one, please,' mumbled James, his mouth full. 'They're really good.'

'It's a lovely day,' remarked Emily Hope, peering out of the window. 'I think we should leave as soon as we can so we don't miss a moment of our day at the sanctuary.'

'I agree!' Mandy got up and took her plate to the sink. James followed, the remains of his second pancake in one hand. He hurried about fetching Blackie's lead and filling an empty plastic bottle with cold water. Mandy scraped a brush through her blonde hair and gathered it into a ponytail, then ran round the cottage looking for her trainers and a bowl for Blackie to drink from. At last, they were ready to leave.

It was an easy drive to Lakeside, along small roads bordered by lush woodland on one side, and a winding river that ran into the lake on the other. Blackie had his nose out of the top half of the window on James's side of the car. His soft furry cheek billowed and flapped as the wind caught it, making Mandy laugh.

Emily Hope navigated from the map on the leaflet Ben Sullivan had given them. 'It says here that the grounds of the sanctuary include two small connected lakes,' she read. 'What a great place for otters. We're nearly there, Adam . . . slow down a bit. We're looking for a turning on the left called Waterhead Lane.'

'Here it is,' said Mr Hope.

The lane was heavily tree-lined. Soon Mandy saw a small metal sign hanging on a broad tree trunk. It featured the silhouette of an otter and an arrow. 'Not far now.' She smiled at James, who was having difficulty trying to keep Blackie from squeezing out of the window.

'It's the smells,' he explained. 'They're different from the ones at home.'

Mandy laughed. 'Maybe he knows he's about to see Daisy again?'

'He must do,' replied James, holding on tightly to Blackie.

Adam Hope slowed the Land-rover to a crawl and Mandy looked out to see a large wooden carving of an otter nailed to one of a pair of white stone pillars. 'We're here!' she announced, snapping off her seatbelt and craning forward to look out.

Adam Hope turned left through the pillars and followed a bumpy track. Just visible through the trees, the morning sun shimmered and bounced off the sparkling surface of a lake. After a kilometre, the track opened out into a tarred, circular forecourt in front of a small whitewashed house.

The first thing Mandy saw was Daisy. The golden Labrador was spread out in the sun, her coat gleaming, but she raised her head and looked at the approaching car. She stood up to give a joyous bark when she saw Blackie's sleek black nose sticking out of the window.

'Hi, Daisy!' Mandy called from her side. Blackie's ears shot up and his tail began to wag hard.

'Welcome!' Ben Sullivan came striding towards them from inside the house. Mandy held on to Blackie while James quickly looped the lead around his dog's collar-less neck. Then they got out of the car to say hello.

'Hi there! Did you have any problem finding us?' asked Ben.

'No problem at all,' said Adam Hope with a smile.

'Can I let Blackie go, Mr Sullivan?' James asked. His dog was quivering and straining forward at the sight of Daisy.

'Sure,' replied Ben. 'Daisy's pretty steady on three legs.' Then he added, 'She's not mad about that thing on her head though!'

Mandy watched as Blackie bounded happily over to Daisy. Her plumy tail waved back and forth, her injured paw held just off the ground.

'This place is great!' said Mandy. She looked across a sunny expanse of lawn to a wide, fast-moving rush of brown water, hoping for a sign of the resident otters.

'Well, we're a bit off the beaten track here but we've managed to attract a few interested visitors already,' said Ben.

'Good,' said Mrs Hope. 'I'm sure in time you're going to be very busy.'

'Come along in and meet Sue,' said Ben, gesturing to the front door of the house.

Right on cue, Sue Sullivan appeared in the doorway, a huge smile on her face. 'Hello! I'm so glad to have a chance to meet you all, and to thank you for being so kind to Daisy,' she said.

Mr and Mrs Hope stepped into the hall and shook hands with her. 'We were so glad to have been able to help,' Emily Hope told Sue.

Mrs Sullivan's hair was almost the same colour

as Mandy's mother's – a chestnut red – and she wore it pulled back into a loose bun. Her cheerful face was freckled and her blue eyes shone when she spoke. Mandy liked her immediately.

'Would you like a tour, then?' asked Ben, flattening himself against the wall to allow Daisy to get past in her cone. Blackie followed faithfully, his tongue lolling.

'Yes, please,' Mandy said eagerly.

'Maybe you two would like to lend us a hand?' said Sue, looking at James and Mandy in turn. 'There's a lot of work to be done and we could do with some help.'

'We'll do anything,' Mandy promised, and James nodded enthusiastically.

'Anything,' he repeated.

'That's nice to hear! Ben and I have devoted this morning to catching up on paperwork,' Sue explained. 'There's still the lunchtime feeding and cleaning to be done.'

'I'd like to take a look at Daisy's paw,' said Mr Hope and Mrs Hope nodded in agreement. 'We'll catch up with you in a bit.'

'Right,' said Sue, grinning at Mandy and James. 'You two can come and meet our residents.'

Mandy smoothed Daisy's back. 'Make sure Blackie minds his manners, Daisy,' she teased. Blackie was standing nose-to-nose with the golden dog. Only his shoulders and back were visible; his head had vanished into the opening of Daisy's upturned lampshade, and two Labrador tails were wagging like mad. Mandy, James and Sue burst out laughing.

Sue Sullivan's first stop was a brick outbuilding used for storage. She delved into a small refrigerator and filled a bucket with chopped raw fish and earthworms. 'An otter's favourite food,' she announced cheerfully.

'Fish and earthworms?' Mandy said disbelievingly. Fish she could understand, but worms didn't sound very appetising at all!

'Yes – and they love eels, toads and other small mammals. They've got very sharp eyes and sensitive whiskers for finding food in dark, murky places. They use their sharp claws for digging up worms.' She handed James and Mandy two long-handled outdoor brooms. They eagerly followed her outside as she began her rounds.

'You're bound to get mucky,' she warned.

'We don't mind,' James told her.

The smelly contents of the bucket slopped from side to side as Sue Sullivan strode along, heading for the river.

Mandy took a deep breath to contain her excitement. She was about to meet the otters of Lakeside at last.

As they drew closer to the riverbank, she heard a merry, high-pitched chattering sound. It came from the direction of a stream that bubbled through the undergrowth before joining the main river.

'Otters like to live in dank places, in the river bank or in reed beds, so Ben and I have built the enclosures as close to the water as possible,' Sue explained. 'We've tried to imitate their natural environment.'

They had arrived at a pen enclosed with waist-high wire mesh. The fence extended into the river, so that the water flowed right through the pen. Sue opened the gate and ushered Mandy and James in ahead of her. Mandy stood still, searching the piles of logs, stones and plants for the otter. Under a stack of leafy branches, a pair of beady bright eyes peeped out at her. Mandy slowly walked forward, following Sue's lead, and went down on her haunches when she was close enough to the animal to touch it. Mandy was hardly breathing, afraid that the otter would scamper away and hide, but she couldn't have been more wrong.

The otter reared up on its hind legs less than a metre away from her, resting two webbed front feet on a round tummy. He chattered loudly at Sue, and she laughed. 'This is Jinx,' she said. 'He was the first otter to come to the sanctuary.'

She reached into her bucket and tossed Jinx a bit of fish. James and Mandy watched, spellbound, as

the otter dropped on to all fours and waddled on large webbed feet to snatch up the fish hungrily. His furry body was just over a metre long, ending in a powerful, tapered tail.

'Oh, he's beautiful,' Mandy breathed. The otter's coat was a baggy swathe of brown velvet that almost looked too big for the small animal inside. On either side of its broad muzzle was a set of transparent whiskers.

'Chirp,' said Jinx, looking longingly at Sue. She threw a second chunk of fish and it landed in the water flowing through the pen. The otter splashed into the water after it, snatched it up, than rolled on to his back. Holding the fish on his chest, clasped between his two webbed feet, he began to crunch happily.

'Oh, he's magic!' Mandy said softly.

'It looks a little bit like a koala bear,' James decided. 'But even more cute.'

'Well, perhaps his nose does,' agreed Sue. 'But that's where the similarity ends. Otters are as quick as lightning, and amazingly dexterous with their hands. They can also be very fierce. They may look cute and cuddly but they're carnivores who can bite and scratch like giant cats.'

'Why is Jinx in the sanctuary. Is he ill?' asked Mandy, who couldn't take her eyes off the animal.

'He's a lot better than he was when we found him,' said Sue. 'He'd swallowed a fishing hook and was slowly starving to death.'

Mandy looked at the eager little face gobbling up the fish. The furry brown tummy poking above the water looked full to bursting. 'Not any more!' she laughed. 'He's as plump as anything.'

'Well, he needs a thick layer of fat under his furry coat to keep him warm. Otters love to swim and play in water. They're what we call semi-aquatic because they spend so much of their life in water. They can hold their breath underwater for up to four minutes.'

Suddenly Jinx stiffened. He rolled over and pulled himself out of the water. Then he sat up and clasped his front paws together over his chest, looking from side to side with great interest. Mandy turned round to see what had caught Jinx's attention. The two Labradors had appeared some distance away. Blackie spotted James and broke into a run, leaving Daisy limping behind.

James gasped. 'Blackie!' he said, going red. 'I hope he won't frighten Jinx.'

Sue shook her head. 'Jinx is pretty used to Daisy being around,' she reassured him.

The black Labrador came bounding over to James with an aren't-you-pleased-to-see-me look on his face. He seemed delighted to have found everyone. Then he spotted Jinx. Blackie's ears shot up and he cocked his head.

Mandy made a grab for him but Blackie wasn't wearing a collar. Quick as a flash, he slipped in through the unfastened gate.

'No!' cried James, lunging for his dog and missing. Blackie crouched down on the edge of the river, his chest and stomach soaking up the watery mud, and stared at the otter as though he couldn't believe his eyes. Jinx gave a warning cry, a high-pitched squeal that startled Mandy. She saw the otter's razor-sharp teeth.

The squeal startled Blackie, too. He scrambled to his paws and scooted behind James's legs.

'Blackie!' James said sternly, bright red with embarrassment. 'Bad, bad dog!' Blackie's ears went down and he slunk back out of the gate, where he stood looking through the wire, wagging his tail hopefully.

'Don't worry,' said Sue. 'There's no harm done.

Jinx doesn't seem too bothered and, as you can see, otters can be just as fierce as dogs!'

Daisy padded up to join them. She was still trying to dislodge the uncomfortable lampshade. She sat down and scratched noisily at the rim.

Sue petted her. 'Let's move on. There are more otters for you to meet.'

'How many otters do you have at the moment?' Mandy asked, as she closed the gate.

'Eleven altogether,' replied Sue.

'How do you get them?' James wondered, using the handle of his broom as a walking stick, so that he left a trail of neat round dents next to his footprints.

'Well, we haven't been open very long, but our reputation is quickly spreading so sometimes people bring the otters to us,' explained Sue.

'Are most of them wounded?' Mandy asked.

Sue nodded sadly. 'Many of them are injured crossing roads at night, although some are just sickly. Our aim is to nurse them back to good health, then release them back into the wild.'

'It's a very good idea,' said James.

'Where do they live, in the wild?' said Mandy, bending down to smoothe Blackie's coat as he walked beside her.

'They dig out dens, called holts, in the banks of rivers, mainly,' Sue answered. 'Or they will take over an abandoned den dug by some other animal. Sometimes they make their holts among the roots of trees.'

'Oh, look,' said Mandy, pointing.

They had arrived at another pen. This one was set back from the river, so it had a man-made pool in the centre. Around the pool were three large hollow logs, and on one of the logs sat two little otters.

'We've put two young male otters together in here – Otto and Splash,' Sue told them. 'Ben and I thought we might one day need to use this pen as a kind of isolation unit, if we ever had an otter with an infectious disease.'

'They're much smaller than Jinx,' Mandy observed. She hung over the gate, smiling at the lovable little faces that looked back at her with great curiosity. 'Why are they here?'

'They were found huddled together when a stretch of riverbank was being cleared for development,' said Sue. 'The bank collapsed under the weight of the earthmoving machines. We were just lucky that one of the drivers spotted the otters in time.'

'Thankfully!' Mandy sighed.

'Go inside,' urged Sue, unlatching the gate. 'Could you help me by washing and brushing out their pool?'

'We'd love to!' Mandy was thrilled. She stepped through the gate.

'James, there's a hosepipe in the corner over there. See it?' Sue pointed. 'You can use that to sluice out the pool.'

'Yep.' James hurried off.

'Great. Thanks, you two. I'm off to feed the others. I'll come back in a bit,' Sue said.

Otto and Splash didn't seem to mind Mandy and James working in their pen. They scurried inside a big, hollowed-out log at first, but soon popped out of the other end, their natural curiosity getting the better of them. Splash began to amble around like a small brown seal, getting in the way of Mandy's stream of water and rolling on his back to clap his paws in the spray. Mandy was enchanted. The otter made happy little noises that sounded like 'hah!' and she felt as though he was laughing with her.

'He's amazing!' she breathed. 'Look, James, he wants me to wash his tummy!'

Blackie had a chastened expression on his face as he watched them from the shade of a tree. Daisy lay nearby, resting her chin on the underside of her cone and dozing in the warm sun.

When Sue came over to see how Mandy and James were getting on, the bucket she carried had been refilled. She poured out a pile of fish. Mandy watched as Otto emerged from the log to eat, holding a piece of fish in both paws.

'They're lovely,' James said softly.

'They look so *well* now,' Mandy agreed.

'Yes, it won't be long before they can go free,' Sue told them. 'We'll let them loose downriver.' Then she added, 'You've done a great job here. Come and meet Sprite now.'

As Mandy latched the gate and turned to follow Sue, she noticed that Otto and Splash had come up to the fence behind her and were peering out through the wire. They stood on their hind legs, holding on to the mesh with their sharp front claws. Mandy was glad to know they would soon be back in the river.

James whistled for Blackie. The Labrador's tail was waving merrily again, as though he was happy that James had forgiven him, but he cast a wary glance over his shoulder at the otters as he went past the pen. Daisy limped behind him, looking demure and disinterested in the otters.

'Daisy was bitten by an otter not so long ago,' Sue explained. 'It taught her to be a lot more careful around them!'

When they arrived at the next enclosure, Mandy saw that the resident otter was shaggy-coated and considerably larger than Otto and Splash.

'This is our Sprite,' said Sue. 'He's not a very happy chap, I'm afraid.'

The otter lay on his back, his mouth open to show a row of sharp little teeth, holding one bandaged paw against his chest. His muzzle was silvery grey and crusted with dried mud. When Sue, James and Mandy stopped to look at him, he didn't move a muscle, although his eyes were open.

'What's wrong with him?' Mandy whispered.

'Poor Sprite lost his mate in an accident,' explained Sue. 'A car collided with the pair a few weeks ago. He fractured a couple of his ribs and tore off a claw. Sadly, his mate was killed.'

'Oh, dear!' Mandy said sadly.

'That's awful,' agreed James.

Sue nodded. 'Even though his ribs have mended,

he seems lonely and a bit depressed,' she told them. 'Otters are very clean animals and Sprite hasn't groomed himself once since he arrived. He's not keen on his food either. We're quite worried about him.'

Sprite regarded the visitors from his upside-down viewpoint without a flicker of real interest. Mandy was struck by the contrast in moods between Sprite and the other, playful otters. As she watched, he scratched lazily at his grey tummy with his good paw.

'It must sometimes make you sad, working here,' said James.

'It is awful when the animals are found struggling to survive – but it's also very rewarding,' replied Sue. 'Our job is to heal them and set them free to breed in the wild. In some parts of the world, otters are on the endangered animal list. We're trying to change all that.'

'That's great,' Mandy said approvingly.

'Let's go back to the house now.' Sue looked at her watch. 'I've saved the best till last!'

James's eyebrows shot up expectantly. 'What's that?' he asked.

'Cubs!' Sue grinned. 'Orphaned otter cubs, just a few weeks old.'

'Oh, how fantastic!' Mandy breathed.

'I've got to mix up some formula for their bottle. I'm sure you'd like to help me feed them, wouldn't you?'

Before Mandy could reply, there came a shout. Sue looked over towards the house. It was Ben, and he was calling her name urgently and waving his arms.

'Oh!' she said. 'Something must have happened!' She began to run.

Mandy and James exchanged a glance, then began to sprint after Sue, with Blackie in hot pursuit. Daisy was left behind, her lampshade bobbing as she limped hurriedly over the grass.

They arrived back at the house in time to see Ben gently take an otter from the arms of a woman. Mandy's mum and dad stood nearby, watching anxiously. A car was parked at an awkward angle in front of the house and the driver's door was open.

'I didn't see it,' the woman said tearfully. 'It just stepped out in front of my car . . . it was too late not to hit it. I'm so sorry!'

Sue put an arm round the woman's shoulders. 'It was good of you to bring it to us,' she said kindly.

'We'll do our best.' Then she turned and hurried round the side of the house after Ben and Mandy's parents.

Mandy and James looked at one another in horror. The sight of the otter lying limply in Ben's arms had been a huge shock. How badly had the little animal been hurt?

Six

Mandy, James and Blackie were right behind Ben, Sue and Mandy's mum and dad as they rushed the otter into an outbuilding at the far side of a yard behind the house. It was an old dairy that had been turned into a treatment room and residential unit for sick otters. It was cool and clean, with whitewashed walls and a few rusty milk churns still standing along the wall under the window.

James firmly closed the door on a curious Blackie. Mandy watched the otter being lowered gently on to a shiny metal table. She squeezed in among the four adults, making room at the table for James. The otter's eyes were closed and Mandy's heart speeded up with dread. Was the poor creature still alive?

She was reassured when Ben spoke. 'She's pretty well stunned, but not fully unconscious.' He turned to Adam and Emily Hope. 'What a good thing you two happened to be here! Will you take a look?'

Emily Hope had found a roll of cloth bandage on a shelf with other medical supplies. 'She's docile enough not to need sedating, but we should be cautious and muzzle her, in case she suddenly wakes up,' she suggested.

Adam Hope agreed. He held the otter while Mandy's mum tied a strip of the bandage around the otter's triangular-shaped black nose. Mandy had a glimpse of very powerful-looking teeth as the otter gave a small shudder and her lip curled for a moment. Gently, she was rolled on to her back to be examined for injuries. Mr Hope flexed each webbed paw, feeling for possible breaks in the bones.

'Are her ribs intact?' asked Sue.

'Seem to be,' replied Mr Hope, frowning as he concentrated on feeling the otter's spine.

Mandy felt a pang of worry. The otter looked so trusting and so peaceful lying there. She loved its small, cup-shaped ears. She was longing to reach out and sink her fingers into the thick, fawn-coloured fur on its head, both to offer comfort and to feel its softness. She watched the rise and fall of the animal's laboured breathing. The otter's eyelids flickered, but she seemed unaware of the probing human fingers on her body.

'She'll be OK, won't she?' Mandy asked quietly.

Sue Sullivan slipped a friendly arm round Mandy's shoulders. 'I'm sure she will. Female otters are always the fighters, in my experience.'

'And there's no blood,' added James. 'That's a good thing.'

'You're right, James. There isn't a wound, and she hasn't broken any bones,' said Mandy's dad. He lifted each of the otter's eyelids in turn. Mandy watched carefully, and thought she could see signs of injury around one of the eyeballs.

Her dad confirmed it. 'Ah, here's our problem. The eye is swollen and has some blood in it. That's where she took the blow from the car.'

'She's probably suffering from concussion,' said Emily Hope.

'Is she going to be blind?' asked James.

'I don't think so,' said Mrs Hope. 'She's had a

very hard blow to her head and her brain is probably a bit inflamed. I expect she has a horrible headache, but she'll mend in time.'

'She'll need to be kept quiet, preferably in a darkened place,' Mr Hope suggested.

'That's no problem. We've got a room set aside that will do,' Sue spoke up.

'I'll go and prepare a holding cage,' Ben offered, 'and see if I can darken the room somehow.'

'Thanks, Ben,' said Emily Hope.

'I'll come with you,' said Sue.

'Why does it have to be dark?' James looked puzzled.

'Her eye is damaged, so looking into the bright light won't help her,' Mr Hope explained. He slipped a needle into the soft skin at the back of the otter's furry neck, then massaged it with his fingers to help speed the drug into the bloodstream.

Mandy felt relieved. It looked like the otter had had a lucky escape. While her parents talked about the sort of drug they would give the otter, she put a gentle hand on the thick brown fur. 'Oh, James,' she whispered. 'She's so soft!'

As James stroked the otter, her mouth opened and closed with a soft, smacking sound. James jumped back and quickly withdrew his hand.

'Shall we give her a name?' Mandy whispered.

'D'you think Sue and Ben would mind?' wondered James.

'Shouldn't think so. What about Belle? It's a lovely name for a lady otter!' Mandy suggested.

'It's French for beautiful,' James pointed out. 'You're right. It seems to suit her.'

'Belle,' Mandy said, when Sue rejoined them. 'James and I want to call the otter Belle. Is that all right?'

Sue smiled. 'She'll need a name if she's going to stay with us while she recovers. And Belle is a fine name.'

Belle's little head lolled as Adam Hope carried her behind Sue to a small room next to the dairy. There he lowered the otter gently into a cage that stood on a table in the middle of the room. Sue had spread an old quilt inside the cage, and Mandy thought it looked very comfortable. Belle lay on her side, with her eyes closed, and gave a big sigh.

'She'll be fine in a few days,' Sue said happily.

'That's great news,' Mandy smiled.

'Now, as she seems to be sleeping off her ordeal quite comfortably, why don't we have some lunch?'

James looked interested. 'That sounds like a very good idea,' he nodded.

After lunch, Sue got ready to take James and Mandy to see the otter cubs. Ben found a bone for Blackie and the dog carried it off proudly, his tail wagging, to a corner of the front garden where he could enjoy it undisturbed. Daisy stayed indoors, resting under the kitchen table on the cool, stone floor.

Mandy had been waiting patiently to see the cubs throughout the meal, and now she was almost bursting with excitement. 'How old are they?' she puffed, jogging to keep up with Sue as she headed for the building where they were housed.

'Just a month or so,' Sue replied, shaking up some milk formula in a large bottle as she walked. 'We don't know what happened to the mother. The cubs were found on a riverbank by a bird watcher, mewing for attention like kittens.'

'Maybe she died,' James mused sadly. 'The mother, I mean.'

'It's quite likely,' Sue agreed. 'Otters are usually very good, protective parents. The mother takes care of the cubs for about a year, and the father joins the family to help with feeding and training when she takes them out of the den.'

The cubs were in an old pigsty in a walled yard at the back of the dairy. As they approached the door, Mandy heard the otters calling faintly.

'They're hungry,' said Sue, adding, 'Again!'

Mandy and James peeped over a waist-high stone wall. There was a large cardboard box on the concrete floor of the yard. Inside the box, the cubs were curled up together in a bed of straw. Their eyes were closed, so that it was difficult to tell where one sleek, dark brown body ended and the next began. Then, one of the cubs opened a hazy little eye.

'Wow!' breathed James. 'They're so small.'

'Aren't they adorable!' Mandy whispered. She could have fitted a cub in each of her hands. They had funny flat faces and small pink mouths, which they opened wide to call loudly until Sue lowered the teat of the bottle into the box. The cubs' tiny noses began to twitch with interest. They slithered apart, raising their faces eagerly for the milk they could smell, making earnest chirping noises like baby birds in a nest. Mandy saw tiny, needle-like teeth as one cub latched on and began to suck. It made Mandy smile to see how eagerly the cub paddled its front feet, its throat working as it swallowed the milk. The second cub had opened its eyes and gave a determined bark.

'All right, all right,' laughed Sue. 'Your turn next.'

'Have they got names?' asked James.

'This is Leo. The female is Eva,' Sue told them, pointing to each cub in turn. 'They're utterly gorgeous, aren't they? I try to handle them as little as possible, hard though it is. I prefer them not to carry the scent of humans when they are released back into the river.'

'Just like that?' Mandy said, not taking her eyes off the otters. 'As soon as they're bigger, you'll be able to let them go off on their own?' It was Eva's turn to drink, and she had a tide of milky froth round her mouth.

'Not exactly,' Sue explained. 'I plan to introduce them into the special holt Ben and I are building downriver. It's not an enclosure but a proper open habitat, so they have free access to the river.'

'That's wonderful,' Mandy said enthusiastically. She looked down into the box again. The male cub's tummy was swollen with warm milk. He curled up in the straw and rolled on to his back.

His eyes closed again and opened only for a second when Eva joined him. She settled herself across his belly, stretched out and yawned, then fell asleep.

When Sue went back to the house to wash the bottle, Mandy and James took the chance to wander round the sanctuary again.

'What a great place,' said James.

'We're really lucky to have it so close to our holiday cottage,' Mandy remarked.

'It was meeting Daisy that led us here,' James reminded her. 'Without her, we might have missed that poster in the post office and we wouldn't have known about the sanctuary.'

Mandy nodded. They'd arrived at Sprite's enclosure, the otter Mandy felt most concerned about. 'He's the sad one,' she recalled. 'The others have injuries that will get better, but this one has a broken heart.'

'He misses his mate,' James agreed.

Sprite lay perfectly still, his eyes blank. The food Sue had put down for him earlier had begun to smell strongly of rancid fish. As Mandy and James sat watching him, there was a gleeful bark and Blackie came tearing through the trees. He skidded to a stop when he saw them, sending up a shower of dirt and twigs. Still, Sprite didn't move.

'Blackie!' scolded James, brushing sand off his trousers. He pushed his glasses up on his nose. 'Calm down, will you?'

'I see a wobbling lampshade,' Mandy smiled, pointing.

Daisy limped towards them, followed by Ben. In her owner's hand was a large metal toolbox. 'Want to come with me downriver to see the holt we're building?' he asked.

'Yes, please!' Mandy answered. 'We were trying to cheer up Sprite.'

'He does seem unhappy, doesn't he?' Ben frowned. 'He needs another mate, a female otter of the right temperament and age. I'm sure the right companion would bring a spark to Sprite's eye!'

He led them along a trail beside the river. The clear water sparkled in the sunlight. Daisy tried to drink, but her mouth was well short of the lip of the lampshade, and she couldn't reach. Blackie paddled at the edge, churning the mud with his big paws, but he seemed much quieter today, as though he was trying to show off his good manners.

'Daisy is setting Blackie a good example,' remarked James. 'Look how well he's behaving!'

'He's having a perfect day,' Mandy said. 'It's turning out to be just one long walk, and he's got his new best friend with him.'

Ahead of them, Ben had slowed down and was crouching on his heels.

Mandy hurried over. She saw a large, level platform made of logs, flush with the ground ahead of them. Underneath it was a kind of den, dug into the bank and going back about a metre. She and James stood at the edge of the platform and looked down into the hole.

'Is this the river holt?' she asked.

'Yes,' replied Ben. 'This is it. All our own design and handiwork.' He stepped down on to the edge of the river. 'It's called a pipe-and-chamber holt,' he told them. 'It's a safe resting place for passing otters and a great start for our own sanctuary otters. Want to take a look?'

James and Mandy jumped down beside him and peered inside. The holt was criss-crossed with a number of long round pipes lying on the muddy floor. They were just wide enough for an otter to squeeze into. The ground underfoot was squelchy with mud and rivulets of water kept trickling in from the sides of the bank.

'I'm glad I'm not an otter,' muttered James, peering into a long, dark pipe. 'I don't think I'd like to sleep in there.'

Above them, Blackie was sniffing at the log roof and Mandy saw him put out a tentative paw to scrape at something lodged underneath. Then he slithered down the bank to investigate the opening to the den.

Ben looked up. 'Those logs are not secure yet. I'm going to rope them together and nail them today.'

'We'll help,' Mandy said eagerly.

'There's isn't much more to do,' Ben said. 'It's a pretty fine holt the way it is but I want to make it safe. It would be awful if somebody fell though the logs into a muddy pit of metal pipes!'

'Awful for the otters, too,' Mandy agreed.

'Too right! Sprite will be our first resident here, I think. We'll transfer him as soon as he starts to eat.'

'Maybe he *will* eat when he's here,' suggested James. 'Maybe he likes toads or voles or water rats better than the fish you give him?'

'Oh, we've tried him on all kinds of delicious things,' Ben smiled. 'He's hardly eating enough of

anything to keep himself alive just now.'

'How sad,' Mandy said, feeling very sorry for the bereaved otter. 'He must have loved his mate very much.'

Daisy stood on the bank beside the holt, looking down at the gathering at the shoreline of the river. She gave an impatient shake of her head, and the lampshade jiggled against her collar. Blackie scrabbled back up the bank and shot over to where she stood, barking joyously.

He began to tear around in circles, trying to encourage his friend to join in a game. Daisy started to bounce along beside him, at a more ladylike pace. She held her sore paw off the ground and hurried as best she could after Blackie as he sprinted on to the log roof of the holt.

'Hey, you two . . .' Ben began. 'Easy now . . .'

But it was too late. Blackie had come crashing across the makeshift roof. As his paws pounded against the logs they began to roll, and Blackie panicked. He scrabbled, frantically trying to find his footing. With an ominous rumble, the logs toppled down. The last Mandy saw of Blackie was his startled face as the roof caved in and he fell with an anguished howl into the den below.

Seven

'Oh, *no!*' Mandy gasped.

She dropped quickly to her knees and began to crawl forward into the den. She could just see Blackie among a pile of pipes and sand. He seemed dazed. Mandy tugged at the heavy pipes and dug at the mud with her hands to free his legs.

'Is he all right?' James called anxiously. There wasn't enough room for him to join Mandy inside the holt.

'He's fine . . . I think,' she reported over her shoulder. Just then, a surprised Blackie scrabbled to his feet, scattering earth in all directions. 'Yes,' she said, 'he *is* fine, James.'

Blackie gave a tremendous shake, then skittered out to the edge of the river, where James and Ben stood doubled over and staring into the holt. The dog's tail was tucked tightly between his legs. Mandy crept out of the den and stood up.

'Thanks, Mandy,' said James. His face was pink with shame. 'Oh, I'm so sorry, Mr Sullivan,' he whispered. He shook his head from side to side, looking, for a moment, as though he would like to crawl into the holt and disappear.

Mandy touched James's shoulder. 'Blackie's not hurt,' she said. 'So that's good, at least.'

'Well!' said Ben Sullivan, trying to sound cheerful. 'That's made short work of that project.' He grinned ruefully at James.

Mandy surveyed the damage. The carefully arranged network of piping was in ruins. The wooden roof had completely caved in, with only a single pole still lying neatly at ground level. Mandy was standing at the edge of nothing more than a heap of beams and pipes, wedged in wet sand.

Daisy appeared on the bank, and stood looking sheepishly down at them. She cocked her head enquiringly at Blackie, and the flowered lampshade tilted comically to one side, but Blackie sat down beside James and refused to look at her.

'I hope you're ashamed,' James told his dog. He had mud in one eye and had to take off his glasses to rub at it.

'Well, I think Daisy egged him on,' said Ben. 'The pair of them were going crazy up there.'

Mandy could see he was bitterly disappointed. This holt was Sue's pride and joy – and it was meant to be ready to receive the otters that were well enough to return to the wild. 'We'll rebuild it for you, Mr Sullivan,' she offered. 'James and I will put it back just the way it was.'

He shook his head. 'That's kind of you, Mandy. But it'll take some time.'

'Well, we're here for a week!' James sounded determined.

'And I'm sure my mum and dad would help,' Mandy added.

Ben smiled at them. 'Well, Sue and I do have a lot of work on up at the sanctuary just now, so maybe . . .'

'Thanks, Mr Sullivan,' said James. 'We'd really like to make up for everything.'

'OK, OK.' Ben laughed and held up his hands. 'Let's go up to the house and tell the others what's happened. I need a cup of tea – and then we'll make a plan.'

'It's not your fault!' Sue Sullivan told James, handing him a glass of iced lemonade. 'Please don't feel bad about it.'

They were sitting in the kitchen, round a table cluttered with a computer, piles of stationery and black files bulging with paperwork. Blackie was lying under the table looking subdued.

'Blackie was just being high-spirited,' said Emily Hope. 'He's mad about Daisy. Perhaps he was trying to impress her.'

Daisy put her good front paw on to Sue's lap. Sue smoothed the dog's head lovingly. Then she looked up at Mr and Mrs Hope, James and Mandy. 'Well, thanks to your kind offer of help, we might still have the river holt ready in time for our conservation grant.'

'What's this?' Adam Hope looked interested.

'We should be awarded a grant by the local council if we develop this as a wildlife conservation site,' explained Ben. 'We're due to be inspected next week.'

'Oh!' said Mandy, putting her drink down with such force that the ice cubes rattled. 'Then we'd better start work right away!'

'Of course. We'll all help,' said Emily Hope.

'I'm in,' added Mr Hope.

'You've been terrific, all of you,' Ben grinned. 'It was a lucky day that our Daisy chose you to come to for help!'

Mandy glanced at James. She could tell he was thinking the same thing as her – if it wasn't for them, the holt would still be in one piece.

Emily Hope looked at her watch. 'It's getting late,' she said. 'Perhaps we should drive home now, and report for duty first thing in the morning?'

Mandy's father stood up. 'That's good thinking,' he said approvingly. 'We'll come back tomorrow, bright and early.'

'Thanks,' Ben grinned. 'We really appreciate it.'

Mandy was reluctant to leave. She kissed Daisy on the top of her head, then slipped out to the treatment room to take another look at Belle. The otter had woken up and her eyes were wide open. She lay on her quilt looking around her. When Mandy approached she buried her head in the folds and tried to hide.

'Belle,' Mandy whispered, kneeling down so she could get as close to the otter as possible. 'I won't hurt you. I hope you feel better. I'll be back to see you tomorrow.'

Belle shifted about in her bedding and Mandy saw the top of her furry head emerge. Two solemn brown eyes stared back at her in the gloom of the darkened room. 'Please get well,' said Mandy, wishing she could cuddle the otter in her arms. 'Please!'

* * *

The next day, Emily and Adam Hope debated whether to leave Blackie at Laurel Cottage or take him to the sanctuary. Blackie had sensed a trip out was on the cards. He wagged his tail as hard as he could and finally won over Mrs Hope by presenting her with his lead. He held it in his mouth with his most appealing expression.

'We can't leave him!' chuckled Mandy's mum. 'He's such a softie. Look at him!'

'He would be very unhappy if he was left behind,' James put in.

'That's settled then.' Mandy was pleased. Blackie could sometimes be a bit of a nuisance, but he was a lovable nuisance and a great friend.

Adam Hope had packed the car with their wellington boots and added a spade he'd found in the garage. They'd put together a picnic lunch, found an assortment of sun hats and were ready to leave by nine.

Mandy stuck her head out of the Land-rover window as they drove along. It was another lovely day and through the trees she could see bright white sails out on the lake. She was longing to see Belle and the other otters, and wondered if Sue would allow her to feed the cubs again.

The car lurched up the long, bumpy driveway of the otter sanctuary. Daisy pricked up her ears when they pulled up outside the cottage and walked gingerly over to meet them, wagging her tail in greeting. Mandy noticed that she was just allowing her injured foot to touch the ground. Definitely a limp rather than a hop, she thought with satisfaction. Spotting her, Blackie whimpered in excitement.

'Daisy's looking much better now,' observed Adam Hope, as if reading Mandy's thoughts. 'It's almost time to think about removing her cone.'

Neither Ben nor Sue seemed to be about so Emily Hope suggested they make their way down to the holt and get to work.

'You be a good boy today,' James told Blackie, as he pulled on his wellingtons. 'And get your nose *out* of that picnic!' He grabbed Blackie and tugged him away from the basket.

'I'll carry that,' said Mr Hope, scooping the hamper away from the Labrador's muzzle.

'I'll lead the way,' said Mandy.

They walked in single file along the well-trodden path to where the river widened.

'Oh dear,' said Mrs Hope, when she saw the mess Blackie had made of the holt. 'He really did wreck it, didn't he?'

James and Mr Hope began by hauling the logs, one by one, out of the sand. The logs were as heavy as they looked and James was perspiring by the time they'd finished. Mandy was glad of her parents' help. She and James would never have managed alone. While her dad and James dealt with the logs, she and her mum fished out all of the separate pieces of piping and dragged them up on to the bank. Then they were faced with rebuilding the gaping, three-sided excavation. The river washed in at the entrance where the sand had crumbled, making the ground even squelchier.

Blackie took the chance to cool off in the river. He lay on his tummy in the shallow water, until he was startled by a large fish.

'Look!' yelled James, pointing. 'It jumped right out of the water.'

'How nice that the otters will have their meals right on their new doorstep,' Mandy chuckled.

'Frogs, fish, water snails and insects galore. What a feast!' Emily Hope called over her shoulder. She was on all fours in the muddy depths of the holt.

Mandy was passing segments of metal pipe to her. Mrs Hope laid them in grooves she had dug into the soil with her trowel to make sure they wouldn't roll away.

'Hello!'

Mandy looked up and saw Sue and Ben standing up on the bank

'You've done wonders already!' remarked Sue.

'Thanks!' said Mandy. 'It's like working in a giant sandpit!'

Above her, James and her dad had already rebuilt part of the roof, placing the logs side by side across the top of the pit. Their hands and knees were muddy and their faces red with their efforts.

'It's coming along,' Mr Hope said cheerfully.

'We've brought you a drink,' said Ben, brandishing a big plastic bottle.

'I could do with a break,' Mr Hope admitted.

'Me too,' Mandy agreed. She scrambled up the bank. 'James, will you give me a hand with the picnic?'

James finished kicking the log he was holding into place, then joined Mandy as she bent down to open the hamper. They began spreading out the sandwiches and fruit. Just then, Mandy noticed that the sky had darkened. A bank of cloud had moved in from the west. It covered the morning sun and the sudden cool was welcome.

Sue sat down on the grass and crossed her legs. There was a distant rumble of thunder and she looked up at the sky. 'Typical,' she commented, rolling her eyes. 'It's going to rain, just in time for our picnic.' Daisy sat beside her. She stretched forward her back paw to scratch the knot of string that tied the lampshade to her collar.

'We should remove that lampshade in the next day or so,' said Adam Hope, watching Daisy.

'She's had enough of it,' Ben agreed. 'Her wound looks pretty much healed now.'

Blackie came up from the river to join Daisy. He shook the water from his coat, showering Daisy with muddy droplets. She went over to say hello, trying to sniff at Blackie's damp coat, but the cone kept her from getting close enough.

Mandy passed James an apple. He was looking at all the goodies they'd unpacked from the hamper, then put out the palm of his hand as the first big drops of rain began to fall.

'Uh-oh . . .' Mandy said. She had taken a can of coke out of the basket, but thought better of it and put it back.

'Those clouds look fairly menacing,' said Emily Hope. She threw down her trowel and climbed up to the top of the bank. 'We'd better call it quits for now. I don't fancy getting any muddier.'

'I'll take the basket,' Mr Hope volunteered. 'Let's go.'

Everybody scrambled for cover as the rain came lashing down. The leafy branches of the trees were bowed with the weight of the downpour and Mandy shrieked as a cold shower of water slithered down the back of her neck.

'This is a shortcut,' shouted Sue, beckoning down a narrow path as she sprinted ahead. 'Follow me.'

Pounding along in her muddy trainers, Mandy noticed Otto and Splash in their pool. They were taking full advantage of the weather, rolling about in the water with evident glee. At least someone was enjoying the rain, she thought.

The enforced break from rebuilding the holt gave Mandy a chance to spend time with Belle. While the others shared the picnic in the kitchen, she took her apple and slipped away.

Belle was asleep but she woke up when Mandy peeled back the blanket that was draped over the crate to keep out the light. She knelt down, her chin on the table. It was thrilling to be so close to the little animal. Belle shrunk away to the far end of her crate, but kept her brown eyes trained on Mandy. Her nose twitched.

'Sweet girl,' Mandy murmured. 'How are you feeling?'

Belle blinked and made a small chattering sound. She looked round the room, but her eyes came back to rest on Mandy's face. Mandy spoke to her in a soft voice, keeping very still. The otter's eye seemed less swollen and, as Mandy sat there, Belle suddenly rolled over on to her back. Clasping her front paws over her pale furry chest, she looked at Mandy from upside down. Mandy was pleased. It seemed a very trusting thing for the otter to have done and Mandy was sure Belle was feeling more relaxed.

'Mandy?' The door to the utility room opened and Belle turned over and backed into a corner. Emily Hope looked in. 'We *did* pack the cheese sandwiches, didn't we?'

'Yep,' Mandy nodded. 'I put them in the basket after I'd wrapped them in foil.'

'Well, they're not there,' said Mrs Hope. 'Are you sure?'

'Absolutely certain!' Mandy thought for a moment, then she grinned. 'Blackie?'

Mrs Hope covered her face with her hands. 'Oh, no!'

Mandy drew her mother's attention to the otter. 'Mum, Belle seems much better. She seems a little playful, even. Do you think she's ready to go into an outside pen?'

'She does seem better,' said Emily Hope, taking a look. 'That's good news! I'll speak to Sue and Ben about the possibility of releasing her. Will you come and give us a hand with making a new round of sandwiches?'

'OK,' said Mandy, leaving Belle rather reluctantly.

In the kitchen, James was gazing sorrowfully at his dog.

'I know I packed the sandwiches, James, so Blackie must be the thief,' Mandy told him.

'Yep,' James agreed. 'Took them from right under our noses!' Blackie looked up at his owner with loving eyes. 'And I'm *starving*, too. What am I going to do with you!'

'It must have been Blackie,' added Adam Hope. 'Daisy couldn't have reached into the basket wearing her cone.'

'Bad dog!' James said sternly.

'Never mind.' Sue laughed, holding up one hand. 'Let's make more sandwiches and say no more about it. Poor Blackie always seems to be in trouble.'

The Labrador seemed hurt by James's tone. He slunk away and curled up very close to Daisy on the hearth rug. He put his nose on to his front paws, but kept his eyes on James. Mandy thought he looked very apologetic.

'Sue,' she said, turning to wash her hands at the sink, 'can we take Belle out of that cage? She really is better.'

'I thought so too,' Sue replied, as she sliced into a hunk of cheese. 'But we don't have a spare outdoor enclosure and she isn't well enough to go free just yet. She hasn't finished her course of medication.'

'Best to keep an eye on her for a while longer, even if she does have to stay in that cage,' Mr Hope advised.

'I've got an idea!' Ben's face lit up. 'It's a bit of an experiment though . . .' He trailed off.

'What?' Mandy was dying to know what Ben was thinking.

'Well . . . how about . . . no, maybe it's too soon.' He rubbed his chin, looking thoughtful.

'Tell us,' urged Sue, looking puzzled. 'What's your idea, Ben?'

'I don't know if it'd work . . .' mused Ben. 'But what about putting her in with Sprite?'

'Yes!' Mandy burst out. 'It's a *wonderful* idea. Belle could be just what he needs!'

Ben grinned at Mandy. 'That's exactly what I was thinking!' he said.

'Belle and Sprite?' Sue sounded hesitant. 'Together . . . as mates?'

'He's so lonely,' Mandy pointed out. 'And she's alone, too. If they get along well, they might team up together and have a family.'

'More otters for the river,' said James. 'That would be terrific.'

Sue and Ben exchanged glances, then they smiled. 'A mate for Sprite!' Sue said. 'It's a long shot, but it's worth a try!'

Eight

Mandy was so excited about the possibility of the two sad otters making friends, she could barely sit still long enough to finish what was left of the picnic. She excused herself from the table and went to see Belle.

James followed. 'You're right. She's looking much happier,' he announced.

Instead of trying to hide, the otter waddled up to the wire, her broad black nose nuzzling it curiously. Mandy was tempted to try and touch her, but she knew that getting the little animal used to humans would not be helpful. Belle stood on her

hind legs and put her furry paws up on the bars.
She gave a small cry and braced her sturdy little
arms against the barrier.

Mandy's heart melted. Poor little creature. One
moment she was running free, her knowledge of
humans non-existent, now here she was cooped up
in a small wire pen.

'It won't be long,' Mandy told her. 'You're going to
be out of here soon and swimming along in the river.'

'Not quite yet.' Sue and Ben, with Mandy's
parents, had come into the room to examine Belle.
Mandy and James moved out of the way to let them
get closer to the cage.

'The swelling has gone down,' said Mrs Hope.
'She seems more active, too.'

'Can we put her in with Sprite, do you think?
Today, I mean?' asked James.

'I think we should try and introduce them to each
other gradually,' Sue replied.

'Let's roll a stretch of chicken wire across the
middle of Sprite's enclosure,' Ben suggested. 'That
way, Belle and Sprite can introduce themselves but
still be separate.'

'That's a good idea,' agreed Adam Hope. 'We
don't want to rush them.'

Ben looked out of the window. The rain had slowed to a fine drizzle and the clouds were clearing. 'I'll need a hand, if you don't mind, Adam?'

Mr Hope pulled on his jacket. 'Sure. Emily, will you and Sue bring Belle down to the holt in a while?'

'Oh, great!' Mandy's eyes were shining. 'You mean now? Good! James and I will help.'

'Put your boots on again,' Sue advised. 'When we've settled Belle, we must get on with rebuilding the river holt, if we can. There won't be a chance to do much around here tomorrow.'

'Oh? Why not?' asked Mrs Hope, as she gathered Belle's medication.

'Ben's going sailing!' Sue grinned. 'He's taking part in a regatta on the lake.'

'Wow!' said James. 'That'll be fun.'

Sue smiled. 'You're welcome to join us, if you like. I think it *will* be fun – if the weather is OK.'

'Adam has always wanted to take part in a boat race,' Mrs Hope chuckled. 'He'll be thrilled to come along and lend a hand.'

'We'd love to have you!' said Sue. As she lifted the holding cage, Mandy's mum had a good look at Belle's eye.

'It's looking fine,' Emily Hope said.

'Great.' Sue smiled. 'Now, let's get this young lady down to meet her prospective partner!'

'Can we carry her?' asked Mandy.

'Sure,' Sue replied.

Belle in her wire cage was heavier than Mandy expected. Her heart went out to the little animal as she heard her whimper and mewl nervously.

When they arrived, Adam Hope and Ben had just finished securing the mesh wiring across Sprite's holt. The enclosure was now neatly divided in half. Sprite had retreated into the farthest corner of the pen. He backed in among a tangle of twigs and logs at the edge of the river, looking glumly at the crowd gathering around the perimeter of his pen.

Mr Hope opened the gate and Mandy and James inched inside. They lowered the cage gently to the ground and went out of the pen. For a moment, Belle panicked and scooted from corner to corner of the crate, trying to find a way to escape. Then Sue leaned over the fence to undo the clip and the door swung open.

Belle lifted her head. Sprite's scent made her nose quiver with interest. She waddled out on to the earth floor of the riverbank and looked around her slowly. Then, spotting the hollow log, she hurried for cover.

'Let's leave them alone together,' said Ben. 'They'll need time to adjust.'

'Right,' Mr Hope nodded. He flexed his arm muscle playfully. 'Who's for a spot of holt building?'

'Me,' said Mandy, a little disappointed that Belle had bolted into the log. She would have liked to stay and watch the otters, but she knew they'd be more relaxed alone.

'Me too,' James nodded.

'We'll need to finish the holt today if we want to go in for that race tomorrow,' Mandy added.

'Race?' echoed Adam Hope, his eyebrows raised. 'What race?'

'It's a regatta,' Mandy's mum explained. 'On Windermere. The Sullivans are taking part and have asked us to join them.'

'That's *fantastic*.' Adam Hope smiled broadly. He looked at Ben and Sue. 'It's something I've always wanted to do!'

'Good,' said Ben. 'It's the least we can do to thank you for all the help you've given us. Are you an experienced sailor?'

'Um . . . no,' Adam Hope confessed. 'But I'd like to give it a try anyway.'

'Done!' Ben laughed and slapped Mr Hope on the back.

'Let's finish repairing the river holt before we even *think* about sailing a boat,' Emily Hope cautioned. 'We need to be ready for the council's inspection.'

Mandy stood up and brushed down her jeans, knowing just how important it was to get to work on the holt right away. Perhaps Sprite and Belle would be the first occupants, as the first safe step on their way to freedom. It was a lovely thought and Mandy had a spring in her step as she followed the others to the river.

By late afternoon, the river holt had its split pole roof in place, and the network of pipes was laid in the ground below. Adam Hope and James had reinforced the mud walls with stones and sticks, to guard against another collapse. Once again, it looked like a perfect little haven for Lakeside's otters.

'This could even be a hotel for otters passing by,' James remarked, dabbing at perspiration on his forehead with the sleeve of his T-shirt.

'As good as new,' Mandy said with satisfaction.

'I can't thank you enough,' grinned Sue. 'Really, you've done wonders.'

'Sue and I would have had to work around the clock to complete this in time,' agreed Ben. 'You've been absolutely wonderful – all of you.'

Blackie wagged his tail as though he understood and Sue laughed. 'Well, I'm not so sure about *you* being a great help!' She ruffled his head.

'Now, go home, all of you!' Ben pleaded, grinning. 'You deserve a long rest. You'll need all your strength if we're going to win that race tomorrow.'

Mr Hope's face lit up. 'I'm looking forward to that,' he said.

'We'll walk with you back to your car,' Sue suggested. 'Ben can give you directions to our mooring before you leave.'

'Can I check on Belle before we go?' asked Mandy.

'Go ahead,' nodded Ben, as he gathered the muddy tools together.

Mandy and James dashed along to take a peep into Sprite's pen. There was no sign of Belle and Sprite hadn't moved since they had last seen him. He was in exactly the same position, in among the branches, with only his sad little face visible.

'Oh dear,' muttered James. 'It doesn't look so good, does it?'

'She'll come out of that log when she's ready,' Mandy said encouragingly. She wondered about lingering a while to watch the otters, but the thought of a hot shower and something to eat made her suddenly eager to get home. 'I'm sure they're going to be great friends. We'll find how they're doing from Ben and Sue tomorrow.'

Emily Hope groaned as she got out of the car at the river the following morning. 'Every bit of me hurts after all that earth-moving,' she said.

'Me too,' James nodded sympathetically and rubbed his upper part of his right arm. 'Especially this muscle here.'

'And my back aches,' added Mr Hope, unloading their picnic from the back of the car. 'All that digging . . .'

Mandy chuckled. 'Listen to you lot!' she said. 'We're not going to be much use to Ben and Sue in this state!' Blackie had found a ball in the car and dropped it at Mandy's feet, looking up at her hopefully. She threw it for him and he bounded off happily to retrieve it.

A hundred metres downriver from where they were unloading the Land-rover, Mandy could see a small boathouse and a concrete launch strip sloping into the water.

'Maybe that's Ben and Sue's boat?' said Mandy, pointing.

'Why don't you go and see?' suggested Mrs Hope.

Blackie, still holding his ball, was hard on Mandy and James's heels as they ran along the bank and down the launchway to where a small yacht bobbed alongside the riverbank.

'*Tarka*,' Mandy read the name inscribed on her hull. 'That was the name of the otter in the book I read! This *must* be the Sullivans' boat.'

A dog barked and Mandy saw Blackie drop his ball and stare at the yacht. Then a golden nose shrouded in a lampshade appeared on deck.

'Daisy!' Mandy cried. The Labrador wagged her tail.

The boat was about five metres long and her sail was folded round a tall wooden mast. At the far end of the deck, Ben was busying himself with the mooring line, coiling a long length of thick rope round one arm.

'Ahoy there!' he shouted, and waved. Daisy jumped rather clumsily off the boat and scampered towards Blackie. Her lampshade rattled and shook as she ran and the two dogs greeted each other as though they hadn't seen each other in days.

Sue was sorting through some lifejackets tangled in a box in the boot of their car, which was parked beside the boathouse. She smiled at Mandy and James as they went over to greet her. 'Hi, you two. These ought to fit,' she said, passing them over.

'Thanks,' said James, taking one and passing the other to Mandy.

'Thank you,' Mandy said. It was a hot day, and she thought she would hold off putting her lifejacket on until the last moment.

'Is there one for me?' Adam Hope strode over, grinning. 'And Emily?'

'Absolutely,' smiled Sue.

Ben and Mr Hope were keen to be off, so Mrs Hope and Sue began to hand their combined supplies to James and Mandy to carry on board. Then, Mandy and James, the four adults and the two dogs gathered to hear Ben's plan.

'We'll use the outboard motor to travel upriver,' he said, 'then stop and have a picnic lunch within easy distance of the regatta's starting point.'

The dogs swirled around excitedly, getting in everyone's way as they prepared for departure. The yacht was a bit crowded, so Emily Hope and Sue offered to walk along the bank with the dogs, giving Daisy and Blackie a good long run and leaving room for the crew. Daisy was hardly limping at all now, and she seemed filled with energy and excitement.

Tarka's outboard engine was fired up and they set off in the direction of the mouth of the river. With Ben at the helm, the boat puttered along under the trees and Mandy scanned the riverbank for any signs of otter holts. This was perfect otter territory, she was sure, and she hoped she might spot a furry head and beady eyes popping up from a hole in the bank.

Looking upriver to where it opened out into the lake, Mandy could see a billowing rainbow of brightly coloured sails, flapping in the breeze. Snowy-white hulls of boats of varying sizes were making for the starting line, marked by buoys.

James yelled to his dog as *Tarka* gathered speed

towards the lake. Blackie pricked up his ears and ran to the water's edge. For a moment, Mandy thought he was going to leap into the river and swim after James. Sensibly, the Labrador chose to race along the bank, barking loudly, and keeping one eye on James out on the water.

By the time Ben cut *Tarka*'s motor and allowed the boat to drift up close to the riverbank, James and Mandy were ready for lunch. The fresh air had made them ravenous.

James was first off the boat. He made straight for the spot under some trees where Sue and Emily Hope were opening plastic boxes filled with home-cooked food. Mandy followed him, shrugging off her heavy lifejacket to cool her damp T-shirt.

'That was great!' James puffed as he joined Mandy's mum and Sue. His glasses were askew on his nose and his trainers sopping wet. Blackie put his front paws on James's chest, leaving two muddy splodges on his white T-shirt.

'Can we have our picnic now?' asked Mandy, flopping on to the grass.

Mrs Hope laughed. 'Hungry?' she teased. 'You'll be even hungrier after the regatta!'

'Emily, have you seen a packet of cinnamon buns?' Sue frowned as she rummaged through the cool box. 'I know I put them in. They were right on the top of the hamper, wrapped in a paper napkin.'

'Oh, not again!' James groaned.

'Blackie!' Mandy gasped. 'You didn't! *Did* you?'

All eyes turned to the Labrador, who cowered under the stern looks he was getting. His tail curled between his legs and he slunk away to find a shady spot under a bush.

'Well, they're not here,' Sue finished, having turned out the contents of the cool box. The rest of the food had been laid out on the rug by now and Daisy came over to examine it all, wagging her tail gently. Then she sat down, and looked out over the lake, presenting a perfect, ladylike contrast to the greedy and badly behaved Blackie.

James looked mortified. 'I'm really, really sorry,' he said to Sue. 'I don't know what's got into Blackie.'

'Never mind,' Emily Hope smiled. 'We've got plenty of food. Nobody is going to starve.'

'Perhaps Mr Hope should fit a plastic bucket over Blackie's head,' James said to Sue. 'That would stop him thieving!'

Sue just shook her head in mild exasperation and waved over at Ben and Adam Hope, who were discussing something on board *Tarka*. 'Lunch!' she shouted.

Mandy couldn't help feeling sorry for Blackie. He seemed a bit bewildered and peeped out at them from under a leafy branch with a sad look on his face. He stayed where he was throughout lunch, and never once even ventured close enough to inspect the contents of the delicious-smelling picnic.

'Right.' Ben stood up and dusted the breadcrumbs from his shirtfront. 'Ready, crew?'

Mandy and James jumped up. 'Ready!' they said together.

Ben spoke purposefully. 'We'll sail together across to the jetty where the race will start. Then, Sue and Emily and the dogs will have to disembark. OK?'

'Aye aye, Captain,' grinned Adam Hope. He pulled on a peaked cap, and Emily Hope smiled at him.

Daisy picked up the shared excitement. She shook her head hard in yet another attempt to rid herself of the cumbersome cone. Then she went over to *Tarka* and jumped on board.

'Come on, Blackie!' Mandy clapped her hands to try and encourage Blackie to board as well but the Labrador still seemed miserable. He took his time, walking slowly towards *Tarka*, his head hanging. Then, at last, he jumped up on the deck.

'Good boy,' Mandy told him, stroking his head. Blackie flopped down, resting his full weight against Mandy's leg as she comforted him.

'He is not,' mumbled James. 'A good boy, I mean.'

Mandy took her lifejacket from Sue as everyone scrambled to find a place to sit. Grey cotton wool clouds were scudding across the sky and a breeze whipped the surface of the lake into ripples. *Tarka* began to creak and groan as the water swelled beneath her.

'Put your lifejackets on again,' Ben advised James and Mandy. 'It's one of the rules of the regatta – no sailing without lifejackets. Plus, it makes good sense now that we'll be sailing on the open water.'

The straps of Mandy's jacket had become tangled. Behind her, Adam Hope hoisted the main sail and it began to fill with the steady breeze. *Tarka* tilted into the wind and glided out towards the wider part of the lake.

'Lifejacket!' James reminded Mandy as he pulled his own jacket on.

'Mine's all knotted up . . .' Mandy muttered. Her hair had come loose from the clasp of her ponytail and was blowing across her face, making it difficult to see.

'I'll help you, love.' Emily Hope held out a hand and Mandy stood up to pass the lifejacket to her.

Just then, *Tarka* pitched sharply to one side. Mandy staggered backwards. She flung out a hand to steady herself – and the yellow lifejacket sailed free of her grasp and hit the water with a smack.

'Oh no!' yelled James. 'Lifejacket overboard!'

Nine

Mandy's lifejacket bobbed away on the water, just out of reach. Everybody stared after it, even the dogs. Mandy was torn. The water looked grey and choppy and she didn't fancy diving in, but without her lifejacket, she wouldn't be able to take part in the race.

Adam Hope snatched off his cap and began to take off his shoes. 'Looks like I'll have to go in after it,' he said cheerfully.

Ben quickly lowered the sail to slow the boat.

'I'm really sorry,' Mandy said.

But before Mr Hope had untied his laces, Blackie

leaped off *Tarka*'s deck and landed in the lake with an enormous splash.

Sue, who was standing nearest the rail, was drenched. 'Oh!' she spluttered. 'What *is* that dog up to now?'

'Blackie!' James shouted. He looked worried as well as cross. The water was deep and cold. Daisy fired off a volley of shrill barking. Her tail wagged madly, and Sue put a hand on her collar in case she decided to jump in after her friend.

But Mandy suddenly realised what Blackie was doing. 'Don't yell at him, James,' she urged. 'I think he's about to save the day!'

Blackie's smooth, powerful paddling helped him gain on the yellow lifejacket as it drifted in the current. He seized one of the floating cords with his teeth, then turned. The water lapped over his muzzle and he coughed.

'Good boy!' Mandy yelled, waving her arms in encouragement. 'Good, good dog!'

'Oh, Blackie . . .' Emily Hope laughed. 'We never knew you had it in you!'

'Come on, boy,' called James. He was smiling proudly. 'Here we are . . . come on.'

Blackie was breathing hard through his nose,

keeping the strap clamped tight in his mouth. He blinked away the water in his eyes as he paddled back towards *Tarka*. At each enthusiastic shout from up on the deck of the boat, his ears pricked up.

Dragging his prize, Blackie reached *Tarka*. The deck loomed above his head, too high for him to climb in. Ben Sullivan grabbed at the lifejacket and Adam and Emily Hope reached down to help Blackie aboard. Sue hung on to Daisy, who was quivering with the effort of trying to break free.

With a great thud, a very wet Blackie was hauled on deck. In spite of how wet and cold he was, Mandy hugged him and planted a kiss on his dripping nose. Everyone cheered loudly and reached out to stroke the black Labrador. Again and again he shook himself, sending droplets of water flying in every direction.

'What a hero!' James declared, wiping his face with the palm of his hand.

Sue accepted a long lick up her arm. 'You're a very clever boy,' she told him.

'You've saved the day, Blackie, but if we don't get a move on, we're going to miss the start of the race. We'd better get going!' Ben handed Mandy her soggy lifejacket and she put it on with a grimace. At least she'd be able to take part in the race now, thanks to James's talented dog!

By the time *Tarka* arrived at the small jetty sticking out into the lake, Mandy could tell that Blackie and Daisy were more than ready to go ashore. A game of tag on deck was out of the question, and both dogs seemed to be longing to play. They jumped ashore after Mrs Hope and Sue, and Daisy's bobbing lampshade soon drew lots of attention from the spectators gathered to watch the race.

'Wow!' breathed James, looking out at the boats spread across the water. Most were small yachts, like *Tarka*. Sails were hoisted as they jostled into position, ready to start. Mandy spotted a lovely little boat with the name *Belle* painted on her stern. Her thoughts flew to the otter, and she wondered how she and Sprite were getting on.

But there was no time to worry about the otters now. Ben was seated at *Tarka*'s stern. He had one hand on the tiller and the other holding a length of rope that controlled the angle of the main mast. A shot rang out from the starting pistol and Mandy jumped.

'Cast off!' cried Ben.

'Best of luck, *Tarka*!' Sue called, and Emily Hope blew Mandy a kiss.

A second later, *Tarka* was gliding forward. She reared up against the swell, pushed along by the wind, and then began tacking from side to side. The water made a creamy froth in the boat's wake and Mandy felt a thrill run up and down her spine. She waved to a girl on the deck of the dinghy closest to them. The girl waved back.

'This is great!' Mandy shouted to James, who nodded. His cheeks were pink with excitement and his hair was standing up in the wind.

The lake widened, then narrowed and Ben and Adam Hope sailed *Tarka* deftly towards the first of the buoys that marked the course of the race. Mandy loved the way the sail billowed and filled with the rush of air. The cream-coloured canvas was so taut she thought it might tear open at any second.

Tarka gathered speed and drew ahead of the dinghy called *Belle*. The first buoy was upwind of their starting point and they reached it easily.

Adam Hope gave a whoop of exhilaration. 'Watch out for the boom,' he shouted to Mandy and James. He pointed to the sturdy wooden beam holding the sail to the mast. 'When the boat changes direction, it will swing right over your heads.'

As he spoke, Ben Sullivan changed course, pulling hard on the tiller as he made for the second buoy. The boom swung round and Mandy only just managed to duck her head in time. James put his head on his knees and Mandy heard him chuckling.

Now *Tarka* was hard on the stern of the boat in front of her. But with the shift in the wind, Ben couldn't get past. *Tarka*'s speed began to drop.

'Oh, no!' cried Mr Hope. 'We're losing our place, Ben.'

'That dinghy is taking our wind,' Ben yelled back.

Then there was another change in the gusting wind, and *Tarka* began to overtake the boat ahead. Mandy's heart thumped as the yacht lurched from side to side. The water splashed up on deck, soaking Mandy's trainers and socks. They were going really fast now, zipping through the marked course and heading for the finish.

'Where does the race end?' asked James, leaning to shout into Mandy's ear.

She pointed. 'Over there – where you can see that motor boat. Those are the judges in it.'

'Oh!' said James, and fixed his eyes on the motor launch up ahead. 'Come on, Mr Sullivan, Mr Hope,' he shouted. 'We can do it!'

The wind carried *Tarka* towards the finish, and for a moment, Mandy thought they were going to win.

'Nearly there!' she cried, and the wind whipped the words out of her mouth. Ben and her father were concentrating hard. There was just one boat left in front of them – a brightly coloured yacht that had rounded the sixth buoy and was steaming for the finish.

Mandy willed *Tarka* to go even faster. She could clearly see the two judges in the motor launch now. She ducked as the boom swiped cleanly across her head, then sat up, just as the brightly coloured yacht crossed the finish line ahead of *Tarka*.

'Second!' she shouted, tugging at James's sleeve. 'We came second!'

A cheer went up from the spectators on the shore. Adam Hope was grinning from ear to ear. He shook Ben's hand and laughed as the sail came down.

'What a crew!' panted Ben, patting James and Mandy on the back in turn. 'Well done, team!'

Mandy was thrilled. She spotted her mum on the jetty, jumping up and down. She waved back and gave her a thumbs-up sign.

'That was fantastic,' said James.

'It was!' Mandy agreed. She turned to her father and gave him a hug. 'What a sailor! Well done, Dad.'

Tired as she was when they arrived back at Lakeside, Mandy was itching to see Sprite and Belle.

'I'll take that cone off Daisy now,' said Mr Hope, dumping the hamper on the kitchen counter.

'Oh, great,' said Mandy. She was longing to see Daisy's pretty face and bright eyes properly again.

Sue was making a pot of tea and Mrs Hope was unloading the remains of the picnic from the hamper. Daisy and Blackie were lying side by side under the kitchen table, dozing.

Suddenly, Daisy stood up and Mandy saw her black nose begin to twitch. She followed the scent she had picked up, right to the kitchen table. Before Mandy could think about what Daisy was doing, the golden Labrador was standing on her hind legs, her forepaws on a chair. In one swift, expert move, she raised her good paw to the table and dragged a leftover sandwich towards the lip of the upturned bucket. The sandwich dropped neatly into the cone. With a deft toss of her head, Daisy tipped it into her mouth and gulped it down, her tail wagging nineteen to the dozen.

'Daisy!' Mandy pointed an accusing finger at the Labrador, her mouth open. 'It was *you* all along!'

'What was?' Emily Hope turned.

Mandy, trying hard not to laugh, explained what she had just seen. It looked like Daisy had found a way to steal food in spite of her cone!

'Clever,' remarked James with a wry smile. 'So who's been a bad influence on whom, I wonder?'

'Poor Blackie has been wrongly accused,' said Sue, stooping to stroke Blackie's head.

Mrs Hope laughed. 'And you looking as though butter wouldn't melt in your mouth, Daisy!'

Blackie wagged his tail, delighted by all the friendly attention he was getting. When Mandy's father arrived to cut through the knots on Daisy's collar, Mandy told him about the nifty theft of the cheese sandwich and he roared with laughter.

'A very stealthy thief!' he remarked. 'Who would have thought that a lampshade would have come in so handy?'

The bright pink lampshade was eased off Daisy's head. Free of the clumsy cone, she went mad with joy. She shook her head for a minute to make sure it really had gone, and raced round the kitchen, knocking over a chair.

'Out!' pleaded Sue, flinging wide the back door. 'Out you go, the pair of you. What a circus!'

Daisy hurled herself on to the lawn and rolled over and over on her back, all four legs in the air. Mandy was so happy for her.

'I'm glad that's over,' said James, as though he had read Mandy's thoughts. 'Now she won't have to keep bumping into things.'

Mandy grinned. 'But I wonder if she'll miss it when it comes to stealing snacks? Now, come on, let's go and see Sprite and Belle!'

They approached Sprite's holt slowly and quietly. Mandy wanted to see the otters without being seen, so she and James crouched down and peered out from behind the camouflage of a handy bush. What she saw made Mandy's heart leap with joy.

Sprite and Belle were snuffling at each other through the wire mesh that separated them. Belle seemed to be making a careful examination of the male otter, starting with his face and working down the length of his body. Then she sat up, blinking curiously, and pushed at the partition with both paws. Sprite chattered back at her.

'She wants to get through to meet him,' whispered James.

'Oh, James, they've made friends!' Mandy breathed. 'Let's watch . . .'

With a jolt, Mandy realised it was the first time she had seen Sprite move about. The apathy and indifference were gone and Mandy was sure she could see a new brightness in the eyes that had seemed so dull before. He accepted the curious attentions of Belle, allowing himself to be thoroughly investigated by her nose and her paws. Then, in a gesture of submission, Belle rolled over on to her back. The top of her furry little head was pressed up close to the wire. Sprite put out a hesitant tongue and began to groom the bit of her he could reach.

'Oh!' Mandy was thrilled. 'Oh, how absolutely *fantastic!*'

The sound of approaching footsteps startled Belle. She shot away from Sprite and took cover behind a log. Sprite, who was used to the presence of Sue and Ben, stayed where he was.

'How're they getting on?' asked Sue in a low voice.

Mandy turned to her. 'We saw them snuggling up together at the wire—'

'And Sprite was grooming Belle,' James interrupted.

'They are friends already!' Mandy finished.

Sue nodded. A big smile spread over her face. 'That's very good news,' she said. 'Ben and I will keep an eye on them for a bit longer, then, tomorrow, we might put them into the river holt together.'

'Our last day,' Mandy said, feeling suddenly sad. Then she brightened. 'It will be a lovely last day and a really special end to our holiday if Belle and Sprite go back into the wild.'

'It will, Mandy,' agreed Sue. 'Now, your mum and dad are ready to go home. They're tired out. You'll have to say goodbye to the otters for now – until tomorrow.'

Ten

It rained all night, and Mandy woke up to the sound of gurgling water. She had been dreaming about the river carving its course through the Lakeside Otter Sanctuary and, for a moment, she couldn't think where she was. She went to the window and looked out. The sky was low and grey. Rain spattered against the glass.

Mandy remembered that today was their last in the Lake District. They were to spend it with Ben and Sue, and hopefully, would see Belle and Sprite make the river holt their new home. She pulled on a pair of mud-splattered jeans and took the stairs two at a time. She didn't want to miss a moment of being at the sanctuary.

James was tucking into an early breakfast while Adam Hope gave the little kitchen a final clean. Blackie sat beside the table, his gaze following the movement of James's spoon from cereal bowl to his mouth. He was drooling.

'Can you finish that cereal, James?' demanded Mr Hope. 'Blackie is dirtying the floor as fast as I wash it!'

'Sorry,' mumbled James. He took his breakfast out into the porch and Mandy grabbed an apple from the fruit bowl and followed.

'Remember,' she said, sitting beside him on the stone bench, 'the day we spotted Daisy lying right over there?'

James nodded. 'A lot has happened since then. It's been a busy week, hasn't it?' He made a face. 'Back to school, soon.'

Mandy nodded and took a big bite of her apple. 'It's been great, though.'

Blackie lay on the wet grass. He had a solemn expression on his face, as if he too knew that he would soon have to say goodbye to Daisy.

'It's been nice for Blackie to have a friend here,' said James.

'Maybe Daisy, with Ben and Sue, could come and visit us in Welford,' Mandy suggested.

James brightened. 'That would be excellent,' he said.

The kitchen door opened and Emily Hope looked out. 'Ready?' she called. 'We're going over to Lakeside now. We'll come back later to pack. Dad wants to get on the road by teatime.'

James and Mandy sprang up. Mandy gave Blackie her apple core and he crunched it happily. Then he followed them eagerly to the car, his tail waving in spite of the drizzle.

They found Sue and Ben down at Sprite's enclosure. The rain had stopped but Mandy could see that Ben had been working outside in spite of the wet weather, because his clothes were drenched. He was holding the wire cage that they'd used when Belle had been concussed. He and Sue were watching the pair so intently they didn't hear the Hopes and James approach.

'Hi,' Emily Hope said softly.

'Hello, all of you,' smiled Sue, turning. 'We've

been watching these two all morning. They're great together!'

Mandy saw that the wire separating Belle and Sprite had been taken down. The two otters were curled up, nose to tail. Belle's broad, silvery muzzle was buried contentedly in Sprite's thick fur. She raised her head and opened sleepy eyes at the sound of human voices. Mandy waited for her to lollop over to the hollow log for cover, but she didn't move. Instead, Belle blinked up at the crowd peering down at her, then idly began to groom Sprite's back leg.

'No sign of aggression?' asked Adam Hope.

Ben shook his head. 'Not for a second! It seems they've taken to each other in a big way,' he said. 'I'd like to think that, by next spring, they might have a family of their own.'

'How wonderful,' Mandy smiled.

'Sprite has eaten an enormous breakfast,' Sue reported. 'He scoffed up his fish and seems keen for more!'

'He'll find plenty of food in the river,' remarked Mrs Hope. 'And the challenge of finding it himself will do him good.'

'Right,' Ben agreed. 'Let's load them into the

carrying cage and take them down to the holt, shall we?'

Mandy watched as Ben pulled on a pair of thickly padded gloves. He stepped into the holt, and Belle began to show signs of alarm. She waddled away from Sprite, making for the hollow log, but Ben caught up with her in a couple of long strides. He lifted her up, grasping the otter under her belly, and she let out a shriek of rage and fear. With one swift movement he had put the terrified otter into the cage. Belle thrashed about inside, calling to Sprite in a high-pitched squeal.

Mandy was sad to see Belle's alarm, but she knew that the treat that was in store for both otters would be worth the scary journey. Ben caught Sprite, who was more docile, with less trouble. His long, velvety tail hung down and swayed from side to side as he was lifted up and deposited in the cage beside Belle. They were a little crowded in there, but seemed to take comfort from being together again. Belle quietened down and stared round with huge dark eyes.

'Hurry, Ben,' Mandy begged.

Ben lifted the otters and walked quickly along the bank to the river holt. He strained at their combined weight, and Adam Hope hurried forward to take one side of the cage.

The river had swollen with the rain and it rushed and tumbled over the rocks, making noticeably more noise than it had before. The water level had risen and Mandy saw that it lapped much higher up the bank, half-filling the metal pipes laid inside.

Adam Hope and Ben slithered down the bank and landed with a dull splash in the muddy water. They pushed the cage deep inside the holt, so that the otters suddenly vanished from Mandy's view. She jumped down to the shore with James right behind her.

Ben reached inside and fumbled with the latch of the pen. The door swung open.

'Keep back,' Ben warned. 'Let's see what they do.'

Mandy crossed her fingers and wished hard. She didn't want Belle and Sprite to make straight for the river and quickly disappear. She hoped they would stay in their magnificent new home, and that she would be treated to the sight of them settling in. She waited and watched in silence, while the river water swirled around her boots, and the drizzly rain fell on her face.

Belle was first out of the cage. She stood aside politely to watch Sprite make his exit. Then, together they set about inspecting the excavation. Belle waddled about purposefully, peering into the pipes and turning over the stones Emily Hope and Mandy had laid there. Sprite stood up on his hind legs, reaching up to press at the log roof and chattering happily. Cautiously, he pushed his claws into the crevices between each carefully laid log, probing mysteriously for something only he understood.

'They're not going to swim away!' Mandy whispered to her mum.

'Not yet, anyway,' Emily Hope whispered back. 'They seem to like their new home.'

The otters explored the entire holt with great curiosity. They popped in and out of the pipes, and to Mandy it seemed as if, each time they emerged, they took comfort from the presence of each other.

Just when Mandy thought the pair might retire into one of the pipes for a nap, Sprite decided to lead Belle out to the river. Ben motioned to the others to climb back up on to the bank and, from there, Mandy had a great view of the otters' first taste of real freedom.

Belle made a soft chittering noise. She waddled into the swiftly flowing water and stood for a moment, looking up and down the stream. Sprite called softly to her in response, as though they were having a conversation about what to do next.

Then, together, they plunged into the water. Standing on the bank above, Mandy watched them glide like velvet brown arrows into the depths of the river. Sue and Ben hugged each other, and Adam and Emily Hope clapped their hands.

'They've gone!' said Sue.

Mandy saw that her eyes were bright with happy tears. 'Do you think they'll come back?' she asked.

'I'm sure they will,' Ben nodded. 'They've made their mark on this holt. They'll be back.'

Mandy looked down into the water, searching its depths for a final glimpse of Belle or Sprite. She felt sad and happy all at once. The otters had gone – and she didn't feel somehow as if she'd had enough time to say a proper goodbye. Her mother and father, with Ben and Sue, were walking away, chatting happily about the success of their first venture.

James stood silently beside her. 'They've gone,'

he said, echoing her thoughts, and he too sounded sad.

'We should be happy,' Mandy told him. 'After all, they're not pets. The whole point of rescuing them is to return them to the wild.'

'I know,' said James. 'But it seems as if they went too soon.'

Mandy knew exactly what he meant.

And then she saw them.

Sprite and Belle had hauled themselves out of the water a few metres downstream. The female otter shook her beautiful coat and scrambled up on to a rock sticking out of the water. Sprite joined her there.

Mandy gasped in excitement and clutched at James. Belle looked back at Mandy with a steady gaze, her warm brown eyes unblinking. Enchanted, Mandy held her gaze for several long seconds.

'Goodbye, lovely Belle,' she whispered. 'Bye, Sprite.'

The otters looked away, and dived gracefully into their watery world. And then they were gone.